Pride Publishing books by C.L. Etta

Single Books
Transcending Phoenix
Mason and the Dog Wrangler

Beyond Heartache
Heartache and Hope
Heart and Home
Hound and Harmony

I0542489

TRANSCENDING PHOENIX

C.L. ETTA

Transcending Phoenix
ISBN # 978-1-83943-811-0
©Copyright C.L. Etta 2018
Cover Art by Erin Dameron-Hill ©Copyright February 2018
Interior text design by Claire Siemaszkiewicz
Pride Publishing

TRANSCENDING PHOENIX

Dedication

Thank you to those in power who inspired me to
write this book. Even more, dedicated to the
hundreds of thousands who fight discrimination
and hate every day.
May the Divinity shine her light on you.

Chapter One

Phoenix Ashe had grown up on the north side of Segratia, a middle-sized domain at the core of Prefecture Staquo, on the planet Gemin. He'd learned from an early age to revere his lineage for its singular preference in matters of the heart and loins. His status had allowed him access to the finest education at the university and prime housing within the city where other Elitists lived and worked. Aware of all his advantages, he thanked the Divinity every day for his good fortune. If at times he became restless and uncertain of his lot, he ignored the urge to pursue a different path. His course had been charted many spans ago.

Each aurora he sat alone at his circular polymer table, surveying Segratia from his pinnacle's crystalline windows and marveling at the beauty of the prefecture's verdant landscape. Watching the sunrise, he often wondered about the world beyond the distant mountains or across the vast sea. *Are the people happy or do they too want something more?*

His rotating sky-floor apartment provided him with an unsurpassed panorama across the city, chasing away the dissatisfaction niggling his conscience. Despite a fear of heights, he occupied the higher-most apartment because it was expected by his parent, his friends and the prefecture's populace. He would have preferred a small flat at street level, something that didn't require an army of robo-servants to keep it clean. Rather than dwell on the simplicities his destiny kept from him, he thought about today's exciting visit to the depository. Fear and anticipation warred within him as he tried to imagine his future. The insistent chiming from his holo-phone interrupted his musings.

"Good morning, Phoenix, my old buddy. What's shaking?"

Phoenix rolled his eyes at his friend's innocuous question. He'd known Gareth for several spans and had never understood how he'd managed to let go of the formal speech that was ingrained in the Segratians. Try as he might, whenever he attempted to mimic the vernacular, he sounded ridiculous to his own ears.

"Good morrow, Gareth."

"So, today's the day. Huh? Going to spurt the Ashe seed into the old stimulator. Have I mentioned, it's like having your brains sucked out through the end of your dick by a robo-vac?"

"Several times, in fact. I don't care what you say, you are not ruining this for me. I plan to be absent for at least a week."

"Why so long? I made my initial deposit in less than two hours."

"I can well imagine. After all, your control over your cock is less than stellar and everyone knows it."

"Yeah, but my refractory period is legendary."

Phoenix scoffed, aware that his friend spoke the truth. The masc was capable of multiple orgasms and *never* missed an opportunity to share his expertise. "Goodbye, Gareth." Phoenix turned off the holophone, glad he didn't have to explain his reasons for his extended depository visit. He smiled to himself before returning to the view out of his windows.

As he sipped his effervescent morning libation, a blending of Staquo's native fruits and its sparkling water, his gaze settled on the southern end of the metropolis — to the area known as Hybridia. The tartness of the drink and the burst of effervescence on his tongue titillated his senses. He wondered if there were similar libations in Hybridia, or if there was something even better. Phoenix secretly envied the Hybridians with their relaxed social mores and less formal elocution. But his parent had ensured he conducted himself as befitting the future mayor. As much as he abhorred the attention cast his way whenever he ventured into Hybridia, the people fascinated him.

Phoenix had often visited the purlieu when accompanying his parent on rounds to examine the maturing fetuses in their incubation chambers. As the foremost physician in the prefecture, it was his parent's duty to make sure the infants emerged from their gestation fully developed and healthy. The infants were then turned over to the parents who, because of their singular disposition, were unable to conceive, thus relying on the depositories and incubation facilities to ensure their lineage. The costs were exorbitant, making it so only the wealthy could afford the chambers.

This afternoon, Phoenix planned to visit one of Hybridia's depositories. His best friend and fellow Elitist, Gareth Knightly, had recommended Seminal Reserve for his inaugural ejaculate deposit.

"Their fellationists suck cock like no others on Gemin. I guarantee, my brother, you will come out of there limp-dicked and totally drained." Phoenix hadn't needed more convincing than his friend's ringing endorsement and after researching all they offered, he had scheduled an appointment.

Since then his nerves had been taut as an archer's bow. He wanted the experience as much as he feared it. Once he made his initial deposit, he was afraid his fate would be sealed. He sighed heavily, knowing it was too late to change his mind. Mintage had exchanged hands and his parent was expecting him to honor the solstice and his station.

The masculines, or mascs, of Staquo followed the old laws of preservation, which demanded the collection of seminal fluids at maturity to preserve the singular elitist genetics of the donor's progeny. Depositories then stored the climatic juices in their vaults until requested by the donor for conception.

Because he had reached his maturation during Gemin's twin solstice, the time when its two moons were at their polar zenith, making his initial deposit during the rare vertex would ensure the purity of his offspring. They would emerge from the incubation chambers with their singularity secured. Mascs destined to mate with mascs.

Finished with his drink and musings, he called for a conveyance to take him to Hybridia. Faster than the flight of the crested ibis, the techno-wonder delivered him to his destination. Alighting from the transport's cabin, Phoenix sniffed the air, taking in the scents of rare cinnamon and freesia. At once his groin tightened, tempting him to adjust his thickening appendage in public, a move deemed inappropriate. Phoenix recalled Gareth saying the aromatics stimulated the singular masc's libido. He'd wondered if it had the same effect on the femmes who lived here or the heteros often found inhabiting the narrow alleyways.

The Hybridians must have immunity to the aphrodisiac.

Phoenix imagined going about the day in a constant state of sexual arousal would be intriguing, but distracting. He put his thoughts aside, noting that his intended destination, on the pristine Inception Promenade, loomed ahead. Since he was early, he found an easy bench to sit on and observe passersby scurrying in and out of the many businesses along the busy wooden walkway.

The freesia-lined walk bustled with enticing femmes—gorgeous, pale lavender skin over sinewy muscles, slender, with silken hair in various bright hues, rolling hips, soothing voices. They walked with the grace of the forest grimalkins, helping him to understand Gareth's fascination with his paramour. His friend had confided he regularly visited a lovely femme who was a depository attendant with exceptional oral skills.

Phoenix leaned back and inhaled the heady fragrances, enjoying the sensations coursing through his body. He had followed the time-tested rituals to prepare for his appointment. His robo-servant had cleansed him within and without. He had maintained celibacy for the recommended sixty auroras to ensure his deposit's purity and he had avoided foods prepared by hetero hands. The proud masc was as pure as a newly emerged Elitist. He breathed in once more, savoring the uninhibited swelling of his cock now that it was free of the constraining ring that had restrained his libido.

"Hey there, gorgeous. Do you need a little help with that?"

Phoenix opened his eyes and surveyed the vision standing next to him. The young femme ran his slender hand over his own tented codpiece, the front closure of his worn pantaloons. The hybrid's shining hair lay over his shoulders in splendid rainbow-hued braids. His lustrous skin shone pale lavender under Gemin's bright sun. He appeared as tall as the six-plus cubits of the Elitists, but Phoenix supposed the illusion was due to his slender frame. The combination of the colorful femme and the pheromones swirling about him elicited a sensual groan. *Stop it! You have an appointment to get to and can't risk wasting your seed while ogling this tempting vision.*

Phoenix scowled as the femme's cerulean eyes danced with merriment and his full lips tilted upward, revealing a smile that at another time would have rendered him speechless. He was laughing at him! Phoenix Ashe, an Elitist of the highest order. *How dare he!* "Are you mocking me?" Phoenix drew upon his emergence-born pride and glared his displeasure.

"No, love. Why would I do that, when all I would like is to relieve you of your — shall I say — burden? Yet, here you are sitting on an easy bench with a strapping and very tempting boner threatening to bust out of your codpiece. When what you should do is walk into any of the depositories lining the boardwalk. Now, what reason do I have to make fun of you?"

"You realize I'm an Elitist, emerged under the zenith of the twin moons," Phoenix said, standing to his full height and puffing out his massive chest, stretching the rich fabric of his tunic to its limits. He tossed his gossamer-white tresses from his face, revealing the black-ringed sable eyes of his prestige. When pushed to the boundaries of his endurance, Phoenix could intimidate the highest-emerged of the Elitists.

"Oooh. I suppose I'm expected to kneel and kiss your over-shiny boots?"

"No, but you should at least acknowledge me and give me befitting respect for my status as the next supporting mayor of Segratia," Phoenix roared. He'd rarely happened upon such blatant impudence in his thirty spans, and how to deal with the offender had him conflicted.

"Well, love, I regret I don't have enough time to pay my respects to your eminence or to what promises to be delectable climax, but I have an urgent engagement. See you around, darling."

Much to his astonishment, the rainbow vision disappeared into the crowd, his laughter ringing out and leaving Phoenix sputtering in the middle of the promenade. No one had ever treated him like an… an…Outlyer, one of those of impure progeny who claimed to be neither masc nor femme. They were often subjected to the derision of the Segratians and had been relegated to the wilderness beyond Prefecture Staquo. This blatant disrespect was why Phoenix rarely visited the questionable neighborhood. Everyone knew a Hybridian's irreverence of an Elitist's purity stemmed from envy. His parent had ensured Phoenix understood the dangers of mixing mascs and femmes. What he didn't understand was why the depositories were all in Hybridia. Prudency would dictate at least the renowned Seminal Reserve move to Segratia. When he moved into the supporting-mayoral role next span, Phoenix vowed their relocation would become a priority.

Double-checking his timepiece, he strolled the three blocks to his appointment, delighting in the aromatic's arousing side effects. While he walked, the irreverent Hybridian filled his thoughts. Phoenix wondered what it would be like to throw caution to the tempest and accept his offer of relief. Gareth constantly praised the talented femme he visited, and loved describing their sexual encounters in detail. His friend often raved about the enticing mouth of his paramour until Phoenix had begged him to cease. Phoenix had been wearing the restraining ring at the time, and the painful swelling of his flesh had taken hours to diminish, leaving him frustrated yet curious. *Would the lavender femme be as accomplished as Gareth led me to believe?* He shook himself free of the dangerous ideas and ventured into the depository.

Cinnamon and freesia punctuated the building's interior, and once more his cock swelled. The scent was stronger in the polymer-enclosed lobby and the effects more pronounced. Cinfree was what the Hybridians called it, causing Phoenix to smile at the obvious misnomer. With the scent tickling his nostrils and libido, his thoughts were anything but sin free. Other mascs sat in the waiting sector, several reading holo-books, others carrying on conversations and a few remaining alone, stroking their engorged cocks. *The cinfree has scrambled my thinking. It's appalling for an*

Elitist of my prestige to use such a coarse term when referring to his anatomy.

Phoenix checked in on the holo-kiosk, verifying he had reserved the Titanium package, which consisted of three phases — inaugural deposit, submission play and intimate bonding. Once he'd received his confirmation, he took a seat and waited to be called. Rather than participate in nonsensical small talk or public frottage, he relaxed and enjoyed the aromatic sensuality.

"Phoenix Ashe? Please proceed to prep area twenty-seven." The telepathically imparted announcement interrupted his erotic musings. With feigned nonchalance, he strolled across the room and down a circular hallway until he came to the cubicle bearing the holo-digits two and seven. He placed his thumb on the digital scanner and entered through the open translucent door.

The space held a nondescript chair surrounded by thick down pillows tossed onto the marble tile. The white floors and walls gave the enclosure a sterile, almost antiseptic, quality. Another entrance, that was semi camouflaged, opened on one wall. Phoenix assumed it led to the vaults. He circled the area, annoyed with his unfamiliar nervousness, and wondered what was expected of him. He ran his hand over the sparse furnishings and touched the sleek walls, shivering at their chilled finish.

"Welcome, Phoenix Ashe. If you are ready, we shall begin. We show you have requested the Titanium experience. An enlightened choice for your inaugural ejaculate," the telepathic voice said. *"If you require anything, your assigned attendant, who is also a telepath, will see to your needs."*

Phoenix nodded, although there was no one present. He was familiar with telepaths and possessed a small ability himself, but he preferred personal interactions.

"Please remove your clothing and place it into the receptacle." A previously unnoticed drawer extended without a sound from the wall next to him. Once he was nude and his garments stored away, it retracted, leaving no sign of its presence.

Now what?

"After your cleansing, you may take a seat. The tele-chair will adjust to your preferences. Your holo-VR glasses are in the right arm. It's your choice whether you engage in the virtual reality experience. Once you're seated and the ion cleansing completed, your oral prep specialist comes in to begin the first phase. On behalf of Seminal Depository, we wish you a memorable deposit experience."

Phoenix took a deep breath, noting the aromatics had resumed their olfactory tease. Delicious anticipatory sensations titillated his nerves and coalesced in his groin. He easily located the ion shower behind a camouflaged panel. He stepped under the polymer showerheads, closed his eyes and savored the pulsing against his muscles as the spray cleansed away unwanted bacteria, safeguarding the purity of his inaugural deposit. When he was done, his body tingled from head to toe, while his cock rose hard and proud from its nest of soft white curls. His lavender skin shone like diamond dust, reminding him of the heather growing wild in the fields outside the prefecture. His pierced nipples pebbled from the cool of the room and the stimulating ions. The silver loops he wore sparkled in the luminous room.

Phoenix took his place in the tele-chair and leaned back. At once the seat reclined, while the cushions inflated, enveloping him within their plush support. He found the holo-glasses and placed them over his eyes. After several breaths, he relaxed as he enjoyed the splendor of the Gemin's twin moons rising through the lenses. His thoughts soon wandered to the pre-inaugural party his friends had held for him. As they drifted, the VR images transitioned into the get-together's carnal scenes. His friends had embraced an evening of primal revelry with multiple partners and near-endless sex. Come sunrise, Phoenix's guests had left him to begin his sixty auroras of celibacy.

With visions of Gareth and himself sharing Temple, another Elitist among their cluster of acquaintances, Phoenix enjoyed reliving the lewd images dancing before him. Paying no mind to the aromatics encircling him but relishing their effect, he stared at his virtual companions fellating each other. For a fleeting moment, he questioned why he couldn't lift his arms, as he sought to stroke his cock. He tried again, seeking to fondle his friend's muscular ass so realistically displayed in the VR lens. After a third try to break free, he began to struggle. *Why can't I move?*

"Relax, love. I've got you." The telepathic reassurance helped him to recall he'd requested restraints for the Titanium package's first phase. He inhaled, savoring the fragrant cinfree. He heard soft footsteps padding into the room.

"There you go, darling. You keep enjoying the pretty pictures and lovely aroma while Tristan Faire takes care of you." Phoenix moaned at the squeeze of a ring going about the base of his cock and beneath his ball sac, remembering part one comprised stimulation and denial, a time-proven practice to safeguard Elitist purity.

"Are you comfortable, love? Need anything?"

"Yes, I'm quite satisfied. Are you the paramour who'll attend me during all three phases?"

"That I am, though we're called attendants. I'll see to your needs through phase three unless something goes awry, and you ask for another."

"I'm certain you'll do. Your résumé is quite impressive and your manager assures me you're the best at what you do."

"I've never had any complaints, love." Tristan's clipped answer and bristling tone gave Phoenix pause. *What have I said to upset him?*

"If there's nothing else, let's begin."

Chapter Two

Cinfree filled the air, stronger this time, unlocking Phoenix's hidden memories. The holo-images resumed with tableaux of him on his knees being fucked by Temple while he sucked Gareth. He couldn't recall the submissive three-way and blamed his poor memory on the hyper-fermented libations provided by the party's host. Because of his social stature, when it came to copulation, he buried his passive desires and seldom indulged them.

The astute telepath attending him read his desires and tightened the restraints, adding ankle bindings. Phoenix's needy moans filled the space, and he flushed at his vocal response, embarrassed at exposing his weakness.

"Don't do that, love. Let yourself enjoy the pleasures coursing through you. It doesn't matter the source. It's your passion, *your* wish — own it. There is no one here to judge you. Your acceptance of your long-denied yearnings ensures the purity of your seminal fluids. Do you understand?"

"Y...yes. But, in my position...no one can know."

"There's only you and me and your lovely shaft secreting its essence." Tristan leaned forward and lapped the fluid coating the hard flesh. Phoenix groaned at the sensuous touch. He lifted his ass, trying in vain to force the paramour to engulf him with his mouth and give him relief from the ache permeating his sac. Instead, the attendant placed a band around his hips, holding him immobile. The telepath promised to lick him raw before he climaxed. Phoenix whimpered and let the delicious sensations course through him as Tristan continued the stimulating tease.

Through the VR glasses, he watched as he sucked Gareth, reliving the orgiastic night's events. He saw the ecstatic expression on his own face as he took his friend's length into his throat and wondered if he wore that same look now.

"You're gorgeous, love. Needy and wanting. I could keep you like this for hours and never tire watching you. You have a beautiful cock, long and meaty, a succulent treat worthy of an Elitist."

Phoenix blushed at the flattering words, knowing his skin darkened with each compliment lavished upon him. Once more the paramour licked him, sucking the head of his erection. He tried to buck at the incredible heat surrounding his cockhead, but the restraints held and all he could do was feel. Tristan tongued his slit, lapping the pre-seminal fluid until Phoenix called out, uncertain if he wanted him to stop or continue. He needed to orgasm, but the ring around his sac denied him. He closed his eyes, blocking out the holo-erotic images, allowing himself to savor the pain of denial as the attendant continued to suck his cock's crown.

Assured his client existed within a state of unfulfilled desire, Tristan laved the masc's shaft, delighting in the way his skin had transformed from lavender to amethyst with his growing excitement. Even secured in the pleasure-chair and bearing an erection weeping for relief, the masc exuded his prestige, much as he had during their earlier encounter on the promenade.

Tristan had recognized his high-emerged client as soon as he had entered the room. The fetching dimple near the corner of his mouth invited exploration. He looked forward to the challenge presented by the future mayor of Segratia. It would be interesting to see if Phoenix Ashe fell in love with him during phase three, as so many of his clients had in the past. But first, he needed to fulfill phase one.

He engulfed Phoenix's cock, taking the impressive length into his throat and keeping it there until genetics required that he breathe. Again and again he devoured the engorged flesh, using his lips to bring him closer to climax.

"Your flavor is that of Divinity ambrosia, salty nectar which makes me thirst for more. I would gladly deny my own satisfaction if it meant I could spend my existence pleasuring you." Tristan sent the telepathic message, deviating from the usual script he followed by personalizing it, employing the more formal and flowery speech of the Segratians. He swallowed and groaned, punctuating his point and praising the succulence and richness of Phoenix's pre-cum until the powerful masc cried out.

"Please, I must orgasm. Now! I'm ready. Please." The ring and other restraints tightened in response. With reluctance, Tristan eased off the cock filling his mouth. After one last tease of the crown he stepped away from the trembling masc and waited for him to settle. There were still hours to go before he'd allow him his release. The mayor-to-be had requested the extended version of phase one to maximize his seed's purity. Tristan seldom rendered a client into the quivering mass of need Phoenix was about to experience. The extended phase would utilize all his oral and telepathic skills to give the haughty masc the orgasm of the Elite. He embraced the challenge as much as he feared it.

He had no doubt of his expertise, and that Phoenix Ashe would get his mintage's worth. What he worried about was restraining his own libidinous stamina. As the attendant, Tristan's own release wouldn't come until they were well into phase two. He had never attended a more stimulating or beautiful masc and, despite Phoenix's superior attitude, he attracted Tristan like no one before him.

With his client's rapid breaths slowing and the subduing of his frantic thoughts, Tristan returned to the chair's footrest. He depressed the lever that held it in place and separated the two halves of the foot rests, widening Phoenix's legs. He sent him a psychic message explaining that he would raise the powerful limbs to give him access to his alluring ball sac. Tristan sensed a struggle within his client and released cinfree into the air, noting the immediate effect the fragrance had on his charge. Unable to help himself, Tristan drank the gossamer strand of pre-seminal fluid which leaked from the masc's cock and let him know how delectable he found his essence.

Tristan kneeled on the soft pillows surrounding the chair and sat back on his heels, admiring the dark, heavy sac before him. The shiny skin stretched tight over twin spheres and he longed to run his hands over the flesh and feel the weight of Phoenix's desire. The contract with his employer bound him to touch his client with only his mouth during the first phase. Entice and deny. The litany played through him as he licked one globe, then the other, listening to Phoenix's entreaties to keep it up — to stop — to do it again.

He laved, kissed and sucked each sac over and over, sending Phoenix telepics of what he was doing to him. With each erotic vision, cinfree wafted over them, and Phoenix's complexion darkened, signaling his growing pleasure. Despite his attempt to remain quiet and professional, Tristan's impassioned moans joined Phoenix's. He kept up the delicious torture until Phoenix once again begged for release.

"Have to come. Please, please. Need it."

Tristan sucked the tender skin once more, reveling in the power he held over his haughty client. He grinned at Phoenix's coarse language and let pride swell through him. Elitist mascs never uttered 'come' no matter how great their need. Instead they asked for a climax, orgasm or for relief.

He backed off his ministrations, breathing deep and steady to calm himself, while giving his client time to retreat from his orgasm's edge. He observed Phoenix, who still wore the holo-glasses, not realizing the visions filling them were those Tristan transported. Except for the hidden threesome memory, the VR images came from him. He sent a brief flash of Phoenix on his knees with himself fucking him. Tristan loved viewing the masc's skin change shades each time his excitement grew. Phoenix didn't disappoint as his amethyst-hued flesh transformed to violet, glistening with sweat and its diamond dust. The results stroked Tristan's ego as he resumed fellating Phoenix's cock and sac.

Tristan leaned forward and tilted the chair back farther, giving him access to the enticing cleft before him. He breathed in the sensual musk and lapped the masc's balls before moving lower to the sensitive skin beneath them. Without warning, he sucked hard and Phoenix's shout rang off the walls. Suck and lick, suck and lick. Tristan played the sensual body like a fine instrument, drawing out the chords and notes of ecstasy.

Before Phoenix could catch his breath, Tristan tongued the wrinkled depression tempting him. Nibbling at the tender skin and sucking up deep, dark purple blemishes on the muscular globes hiding the entrance into Phoenix's body, he feasted on the flesh before him, fighting the urge to probe him and savor his passionate heat. Tristan widened the leg rests, stretching Phoenix open as far as the chair allowed. Phoenix's body undulated within the limits of the bindings and darkened with each tease as Tristan stabbed him with his tongue. His lust filled cries resonated in the warm chamber, while in his mind, he saw his own pale lavender cock pounding into the plum-colored Elitist. He flashed Phoenix a telepic of his own wishful imaginings. *Oh, my Divinity. I didn't intend to do that.*

"Yes, Please I beg you. Fuck me!" *Soon, love.* Tristan thought of their first contentious meeting on the promenade to squelch his overactive telepathy. Once he had his thoughts under control, he repeated the carnal assault on Phoenix's body, beginning with cinfree, then oral cock stimulation, moving on to ball tease, followed by anal titillation. He kept Phoenix on the edge, noting the room's rising temperature and condensation clinging to the walls.

Bathed in sweat, Phoenix writhed in the chair, his cock leaking and pooling its pre-seminal fluid beneath him. Try as he might, Tristan could not keep up with the copious flow. The masc's sweat-dampened hair clung to his face. Tristan fought the urge to brush it away from his elegant features, wishing to see his client's passion-filled eyes. White tendrils glistened against his wine-hued skin, making it appear nearly black under the cubicle's diffused lighting.

"I beseech you, in the name of the Divinity, let me come," Phoenix begged.

"We're almost there, love. Trust me, Tristan Faire knows what you need," he said before tightening the ring encircling Phoenix's cock and starting again with fellatio. Cock, balls, taint, hole. He repeated the pattern over and over, sucking on his client's overstimulated pelvis until he no longer saw his marks on the near ebony skin.

Black-orchid. The shade that signaled Phoenix's step across the threshold of lust into procreation oblivion. His seminal fluids were ready, roiling with the spermatozoa-rich intoxicant. Tristan fought the urge to remove the containing ring and drink his fill of the masc's emissions. To hijack an Elitist's inaugural deposit was an imprisoning offense, according to the old laws. Despite the threat of punishment, he was tempted to discover if the rumors were true. The spend from a masc of Phoenix's prominence would taste like sweet grapes and gift him with elitist stature. *Is that what I want? I've never thought so, but then –* "Tristan!" The desperate shout mobilized him into closing the gates on his felonious thoughts. With one last lap from Phoenix's flowing cock, he rose and pressed a panel on the wall which opened a hidden cabinet.

He withdrew a transparent hose, making certain there were no bends or folds in the pliable material. He placed the open end over the engorged erection, enjoying his client's mewling whimper at the tube's touch. He tightened it at the cock's base and removed the containing ring. Another burst of cinfree filled the air, eliciting a small groan from Phoenix.

"Give it a moment to adjust to your girth, love." Tristan teleported the message to his charge, along with a quick flash of him fellating his massive cock. The erotic image made Tristan's balls ache from the hours spent teasing his client. He was more than ready for his own release.

"Close your eyes, darling, and don't open them until I give the command."

Phoenix nodded. Tristan removed the VR lenses and positioned him and his hose-encased cock so Phoenix could see the climaxes. Tristan licked his swollen lips, knowing he'd done his job well and the results would be spectacular.

He pressed the remote he held in his hand. Warm lubricant poured over Phoenix's cockhead from the tube. He whimpered as the suction started, the noises he made sounding delirious with lust. The apparatus had been meticulously designed to simulate Tristan's mouth. With the visions he was sending the masc, Phoenix would be unable to tell that the stimulator was milking him. Until he opened his eyes, he'd believe his attendant was still fellating him.

With each draw of the hose, Phoenix cried out his need to come. Tristan released the bindings around his torso and delighted in the frantic dance of the Elitist's powerful hips. He thrust upward, trying in desperation to spill his seminal fluids, but Tristan held the control. He stared as sweat poured off Phoenix's skin, the diamond dust shining bright against the black-orchid flesh. He pressed the remote again and the suction increased. Tristan transmitted visions of himself hollowing his cheeks and sucking his client's mighty cock.

"Oh, Divinity. Fuck me. Tristan. Fuck, fuck!" Tristan responded by increasing the stimulator's pull. "Oh sweet, Divinity. Now, please. Come… I have to fucking come. Divinity, I *beg* you."

"Open your eyes, love," Tristan commanded at the same time as he tightened the constraining hold and increased the suction.

Phoenix opened and blinked at his surroundings. His cock was longer, thicker and darker than he'd ever seen it. His slit shimmered with his juices. The pressure and heat from the clear encasement felt phenomenal. He watched, fascinated, as the stimulator pumped him to the point of insanity. Somehow, he had enough presence of mind to realize Tristan still controlled his release. He wondered where his paramour had disappeared to and turned his head to locate him.

"No, love. We're almost there. You don't want to miss your inaugural deposit. Keep your eyes on your gorgeous self."

The heat and suction increased, and Phoenix thrust his hips upward, mindlessly fucking the crystalline tubing surrounding him. Without warning the tube's base loosened, cinfree filled his senses and he screamed. "Fuuuuccckkk!" Brutal spasms gripped his body as he shot thick streams of sparkling seminal fluid into the stimulator. The eruptions went on and on until Phoenix wondered if he would survive the orgasm. Exhausted, he longed to shut his eyes and rest, but couldn't tear his gaze away from the purity of his seed. His future progeny would develop from this, his inaugural deposit, harvested during the twin moon solstice. Pride permeated his soul as he continued ejaculating into the relentless maw.

"Tristan?"

More cinfree surrounded him. And though he wasn't ready, his cock hardened and darkened within the stimulator's grip.

"Easy, love. That's just the first. You contracted for five. We can't stop until we've done the job." Tristan transmitted another tableau, this one from the memories of the masc's pre-inaugural party. Once again Phoenix was on his knees, with Temple fucking him. Phoenix groaned and let the erotic sensations overtake him until he was once again shouting and spilling into the stimulator. Fascinated, he observed his seminal fluids disappear into the receptacle at the other end of the hose until cinfree and erotic images captured his attention once more.

Tristan kept watch as three more climaxes exploded from Phoenix's worn body, each one as powerful and impressive as the first. He had to admit, observing the seminal fluid shooting into the hose was intoxicating. The spermatozoa sparkled in the dim lights like tiny fireflies. With each subsequent orgasm, Phoenix's skin darkened and Tristan sent him visions of himself fucking the future mayor. Pale lavender flesh pounding into his Elite, black-orchid stained ass. *Soon, sweet thing. I'll kiss you and your delightful dimple. You'll belong to me.*

Chapter Three

Phoenix awoke between cool sheets on a bed filled with clouds. He stretched his arms over his head, savoring his muscles' slight ache. When he noticed the mottling of his skin, he smiled with satisfaction and recalled the previous day spent strapped in the pleasure-chair. He'd lost count of the number of times he'd orgasmed as he exultantly spilled his seed into the depository. For his coloring to take this many hours to revert to its usual iridescent lavender, his paramour's talent had been extraordinary. Because of the attendant's skill, his singular essence was now safeguarded and stored away—his Elitist line preserved.

Phoenix closed his eyes and tried to imagine what Tristan looked like. *Did he put me to bed when we were done?* He remembered nothing of what had happened after his fifth—or was it the sixth—orgasm? The visions he'd had of Temple fucking him comprised the majority of yesterday's memories. They were lascivious images of his friend's dark cock, pounding his wine-flushed ass, telepathic pictures forced upon him by the skilled paramour. They were enticing, but the scene that stood out was of a pale lavender lover riding his black-orchid flesh. Phoenix longed to throw caution to the tempest and allow the forbidden encounter. But as the future mayor of Segratia, he kept his unacceptable desires to himself. Mascs fucked or fellated. Period. They were never fucked, according to the social mores of the day.

Which was why he had contracted for the Titanium package. Once he recuperated from phase one, he would treat himself to a week's long commitment to indulge his submissive nature. He hoped the paramour was just as talented in the role of a Dominant as he had been in the depository. As Phoenix pictured the possibilities open to him, his skin tingled.

He rose from the bed and located the evacuation room. Once he'd relieved and cleansed himself, he stepped into the ion shower and set the controls to massage. The soothing spray worked the stiffness from his muscles and the tenderness from his groin. As promised, his attendant had licked him raw. He looked down, startled at the dark bruises marring his lavender flesh. *The paramour possesses a mouth unlike anyone I've encountered. Too bad he can't return to Segratia with me.*

His morning ritual completed and his forbidden thoughts tucked away, he strode nude into the bedroom to discover Seminal's staff had delivered his morning repast. In the alcove overlooking the promenade stood a small table. An effervescent libation rested next to a covered salver, piquing Phoenix's curiosity. He picked up the crystal glass and sipped the drink, happy to taste the tart flavor and sparkling bubbles. *Ah, Staquo's water. Excellent.* Unable to stave off his inquisitive nature, he lifted the salver's lid. The tray held a jar filled with an ointment, a constraining ring, a tiny box and a handwritten missive. He opened the folded paper, sat and read the contents.

Good daybreak, Phoenix Ashe. I trust you slept well and all your expectations for phase one were met to your complete satisfaction. If so, we will proceed to phase two. I've been informed your safe words are "sterling" to slow down and "ibis" to stop. Rest assured, if you use them, I will honor them.

Your morning libation is enriched with supplements to satisfy your nutritional needs and boost your body's healing of any lingering or unpleasant effects from your time in the pleasure chair. When you have finished the drink, open the box and remove the chain within. Attach the ends to your nipple rings, then lie on the bed and fondle your gorgeous cock until you obtain full erection. Once you're ready, put on the containing ring. Finally, please take the jar's ointment and apply a liberal amount to your anal channel.

When you've finished, follow the aqua lights.
Tristan Faire

With a mixture of trepidation and anticipation, Phoenix finished the drink and noted that his skin had lost its mottling and the bruises had faded. He opened the container's lid to find a sparkling chain in a nest of freesia petals and shaved cinnamon bark. The aromatics stirred his libido, and though he thought it an impossibility, his cock began to thicken. He lifted the body jewelry and admired the craftsmanship. Hanging from the center link, a small engraved coin proclaimed the wearer belonged to Tristan Faire. Conflicted about whether to be angered at the paramour's audacity or pleased at his ownership claim, he fastened the delicate loops to his rings. He rose, and with the cinfree filling his senses and the pull on his nipples, his cock stood erect. Phoenix strode about the room, savoring the electric sensations firing from the loops to his balls as he tugged the chain.

"I'm waiting. Get on with your preparation." Tristan's authoritative voice echoed in his head.

Telepaths. Never a free thought with them nearby.

Phoenix swore he heard laughter but scrambled to follow the missive's directions. He debated whether to fondle himself as instructed since he had already achieved a full erection, but determined that if he didn't, Tristan would know. He used a bit of the cinfree-scented lubricating ointment and wrapped his hand around his shaft. After three tugs, he needed relief. Groaning with frustration, he retrieved the restraining ring and snapped it in place.

Not wanting to keep Tristan waiting any longer, he took the jar, dipped his finger in the viscous lubricant and applied it, noting how his breathing quickened as he fingered his channel. Wanting to orgasm from the stimulating combination of the cinfree and penetration, Phoenix mewled and considered removing the ring.

"Don't, Phoenix Ashe." The telepathic warning stopped him. *"You are ready, now join me. I'm waiting and I dislike waiting."* Phoenix looked for a kaftan or some other clothing article but found none. *"Hurry!"*

The command from Tristan was indisputable so Phoenix had no option but to leave his room and stride naked through the unfamiliar maze of hallways. Peering out of the door, he was pleased to see no one around. He stepped out and followed the small aqua arrows lighting his way. With each step, his long, hard cock swayed back and forth, silver strands of pre-ejaculate dripping and leaving a trail. The nipple-chain's pendant pulled on the rings and every enticing sensation settled in his groin. He couldn't tell in the dim halls, but he was certain his skin had darkened.

The glowing bulbs led him to a quiet octagonal room filled with a variety of Segratians and Hybridians, all in various stages of undress and arousal. Mascs wearing containing rings or femmes adorned with lavish and glittering chains and jeweled anal plugs, they were a tempting cornucopia of carnality. As he stared, wondering what he should do next, flashing aqua lights drew his attention. He walked toward the luminous cubicle of translucent polymer, noticing other mascs seated in similarly lighted nooks, their darkened cocks erect and leaking pre-ejaculate. He took his cue from them and sat on the plain white stool inside the panels. He waited with his feet flat on the warm floor and his back straight. Phoenix stroked his cock, thinking about his paramour. As his excitement grew, he fisted it harder and faster, trying to relieve himself despite the containment ring.

"Don't move, love. Your body belongs to me." Tristan's telepathic command broke through Phoenix's frenzied lust. *"What I do with it is for my pleasure and my will. Now, let me have your safe words."*

"St…sterling to pause and ibis to stop. Do I get to see you?"

"Only if it's my choice, love. Now, breathe deep and slow."

Phoenix followed his attendant's instructions and moaned as cinfree suffused the air. With each inhalation, he floated on a precipice of unfulfilled desire. His eyelids fluttered closed and he let his mind drift. Cerulean eyes ringed with dark lashes watched him. They seemed familiar, but before he could recall where he'd seen them, the image vanished, leaving him disappointed and unsettled.

"I enjoy watching you like this, darling. You are exquisite with your diamond-dusted skin glistening and changing shades. Your cock's begging for attention. Let's see if it likes Dorian."

One of the femmes, with a smaller build and soft features, knelt before him, his sensual adornments glittering and undulating with each graceful motion. His erect cock had a gold bead sitting in the slit with several fine chains dangling from it and tickling his depilated ball sac. Phoenix fixated on the tiny sphere. The femme leaned back, grasped his ankles and lifted his hips, fucking the air with sublime grace.

"Lovely, isn't he?"

"Yes." *Praise the Divinity, for he is magnificent.* Phoenix continued staring, mesmerized by the display before him. Dorian paused and turned, giving Phoenix a view of the ornament penetrating him. An aquamarine jewel the size of an ibis egg sparkled from between his butt cheeks. With his ass high in the air, he reached around and fucked his channel with the dazzling plug. Dorian's lusty groans and quivering undulations had his one-masc audience longing for more than voyeuristic observance. He stopped his erotic dance and crawled to Phoenix, slithering up his massive frame, taking the nipple chain pendant between his lips and pulling. Lust, hot and fierce, coursed through Phoenix's body. Crazed with desire, he rutted against Dorian, somehow knowing he shouldn't grasp him no matter how much he wanted to. He gripped the stool's edge and gritted his teeth.

"Lovely. Remember, it's my wish that you remain still, even though you're tempted to do otherwise." Tristan's telepathic reminder helped with maintaining his composure.

Phoenix stopped his movements and panted, willing his overstimulated body to calm. When he was once again placid, Dorian knelt before him. His wicked smile should have warned Phoenix, but he shouted when Dorian took his weeping cock between his lips and sucked it, regardless of Phoenix begging him to stop. His muscles quivered with the effort it required to sit still and not give in to his desire to fuck that luscious mouth.

Preoccupied with obeying Tristan's telepathic order to remain motionless, Phoenix startled when the seductive femme grasped his cock and secured a series of gold rings under the crown and around his shaft. Several fine chains linked between aquamarine jewels dangled from the last circlet and tickled his balls.

"Stand, please," Dorian said, his silken voice adding to his allure. The bejeweled femme encircled Phoenix's waist and fastened a gilded belt like the one he wore. He then ran filigree threads through the eyelets on the rings and secured the ends to the ring in the center of the girdle, ensuring his cock pointed skyward.

"Stunning work, Dorian Seaborn. I am pleased, but I believe our masc could use a little more sparkle." Though Tristan spoke to the femme, Phoenix heard him through their telepathic link.

Dorian licked his full lips and smiled before inserting a short, jewel-tipped wand into his slit. Phoenix shuddered, the sensation of orgasm flowing through him. He flushed and stared at the aqua jewel resting in his cock, uncertain whether he liked it.

"Gorgeous. It compliments your violet hue, but I believe we're in the mood for plum today. What do you think, Dorian? Do you have something to bring out his color?"

"I do, Tristan Faire."

"*Turn and bend from the waist. Hold on to the stool and keep your eyes open,*" Tristan said. Phoenix turned and saw that the cubicle's panels now reflected his image. He leaned over and held on to the seat's edges, staring at the gem twinkling in his cock. "*When you're ready, Dorian.*"

In his position, he recognized what was coming, but still he flinched when Dorian touched him. Tristan's voice came through their link as he tried to comfort him. "*Easy, love. Remember you prepped yourself earlier for this. Breathe and let Dorian take care of you.*"

Again, Dorian's light touch circled his puckered flesh, and though he'd been penetrated before, he had never worn an anal plug. The thought of a second foreign object inserted into him was daunting. He inhaled and watched his reflection as his skin glistened with sweat.

"Look, Phoenix. Isn't it splendid? You're a very fortunate masc to have Tristan Faire looking after you."

He met Dorian's gaze in the reflective glass. His eyes widened at the size of the aquamarine stone he held. The gem sparkled like a thousand stars atop the daunting probe. Mesmerized, Phoenix could not look away as the pretty femme fellated the bulbous plug. Phoenix thrust his hips and groaned as the chains caressed his sensitive balls.

"*Dorian, our masc is becoming restless. Let's not keep him waiting, sweets.*"

Dorian put the saliva-coated plug against Phoenix's opening and slowly inserted it until the first bulb disappeared. He paused. Phoenix gripped the seat, the corded muscles of his powerful arms trembling as he pleaded with his body to relax and accept the intrusion. Phoenix panted through the burn and stretch of his opening and groaned when Dorian resumed situating the plug. As the second and larger bulb filled him, he opened his mouth to use his safe word but cinfree filled his senses as Dorian added more lubricant. Phoenix could only moan through the sensual intrusion. His legs trembled as the femme pushed the largest bulb, into his expanded channel. "Oh Divinity! It burns. Please, stop. I beg you. Stop!" Sweat dripped from his taut muscles as he quivered in pain and pleasure.

"You're doing beautifully, Phoenix Ashe. Open your eyes. Witness yourself and what you are taking for me. See what I see. The lovely plum shade of your flesh, shimmering in carnal glory, your glorious cock displaying my jewelry like no other before you. You are exquisite, so powerful and so needy." Phoenix stared at his reflection, not recognizing himself. Gone was the haughty and confident mayor-to-be. His eyes were large and black, glowing with excitement. *"Make him scream, Dorian."*

"What? Wait! What does he mean?"

Dorian removed the plug and pushed it back in, fucking his charge mercilessly. Phoenix shuddered with each thrust of the probe, his cock jumping and twitching, trying in vain to orgasm. He needed relief and he needed it *now*. "Please, Dorian. I beg you."

Dorian responded by leaving the plug seated deep in Phoenix's channel and fucking his cock with the jeweled wand. Phoenix's vision blurred as he was driven to near insanity. When Dorian pressed hard on the aquamarine plug he howled, shouting and begging to come.

"Open your eyes, love," Tristan's smooth voice commanded.

His wine-colored cock strained at the rings encircling it. The jewel winked in his slit, taunting him. His mouth hung open as he drew in air, saliva dripping from one corner. He chest rose with each rapid breath, causing the golden chains to dance and tug at his sensitive nipples. The lewd image was unrecognizable as Phoenix Ashe, Elitist masc.

"All right, my lovelies. I believe we're ready to go out. Dorian, put on his mask and guide him to the promenade exit. I'll meet you there. Do what you must to ensure his plum coloring doesn't fade away."

"Praise the Divinity. Tristan's taking us out for the display parade! All of Hybridia will be there to admire our hedonistic decadence."

"What exactly is this exhibition? And why must I wear a mask?"

"Well, that's an easy one. Because Tristan wants you disguised. It's his will. As for the parade, it gives the depository attendants like Tristan and myself recognition for the important work we do."

"Important? Your station is just above that of a paid courtesan."

"And yet who sought us out when he wanted to ensure his precious Elite lineage?"

"For the depository—somewhere to store my essence."

"Foolish masc. If that was all you wanted, you could have brought in a spend flask and paid for storage. Don't deceive yourself and don't lie to me or Tristan."

"It's just that—"

"Fuck me raw from behind!" Phoenix startled at Dorian's coarse expletive, wondering what had brought it on.

"What? What's wrong?"

"Look at you. You have turned violet!"

"So?"

"Tristan will demote me and find another to help him if you lose the plum. Turn around and bend over. Hurry."

"I don't—"

Faster than he believed possible, Dorian spun him and shoved him over the stool. He'd angered the femme, but he was uncertain what he'd done. Before he could dwell on his misdeed, an over-abundance of cinfree filled the air and Dorian covered his eyes with a mask delivered by another pretty femme, who advised them to be quick.

Despite the mask covering his eyes and Dorian's displeasure with him, the femme soon had his erection throbbing and weeping. "Please, for pity's sake. I need to come! Please."

"I'm waiting, Dorian!" Though Tristan's irritation was directed at the attendant, Phoenix heard his call through their telepathic link.

After Dorian had attached a short aquamarine-encrusted leash to the nipple chain, he escorted Phoenix through the eight-sided preparation chamber toward the exit to meet Tristan. Each time Phoenix faltered, Dorian pulled hard on the tether, demanding he keep up.

"Courtesan, indeed!" Dorian's resentment was evident with each tug, making Phoenix regret taunting the femme.

Chapter Four

Amused, Tristan watched as Dorian and Phoenix joined him. Unabashed, he'd listened in on their argument and realized the mayor-to-be would pay for insulting his proud friend. Seeing Phoenix flinch each time Dorian tugged his leash clued him in on Dorian's revenge. Their jobs as the premier femme attendants in Hybridia were a source of pride for them, but Dorian thrived on the notoriety. Today's parade would add to their acclaim.

"You're both lovely. Excellent work, Dorian," Tristan said, deepening his voice so Phoenix wouldn't recognize him. He'd already shown the man his unique eyes in a telepathic vision. He wasn't yet ready to reveal himself.

Other mascs and femmes milled around the courtyard, where they waited for the parade to begin. The depositories held the event every sixty auroras, and this one was special, taking place during the twin solstice. If the Hybridia populace voted him and Dorian Most Illustrious Attendants, they would be elevated from their current position to depository pleasure mentors. No more servicing haughty, unappreciative mascs on their knees until their joints screamed in pain and their lips bled. He and Dorian often worked together as a team, to minimize their discomforts and to extend their longevity as attendants, on occasion sharing a bed when they could no longer ignore their own need for relief.

"They're ready to go," Dorian said, pulling on Phoenix's leash. The camouflaged masc whimpered, yet his flushing skin belied his discomfort.

"You really are exquisite, Phoenix Ashe. Come, let us begin. You will follow me while Dorian keeps you interested from the rear." Tristan chuckled at his little pun and tossed his rainbow-hued braids, wishing they'd had time to brush Phoenix's white tresses until they shone brighter than the galaxy's luminous stars. He looked forward to phase three of their contract, when he would wrap himself in the gossamer curtain while Dorian went on his holiday, leaving him alone with the magnificent masc. Putting aside his desires, Tristan sent Phoenix a message that they were ready to start and, although he wore a mask, he would see all that was happening through telepathic visions.

"Th…thank you. I appreciate your kindness."

"Don't thank me yet. The parade and presentation will be difficult for you. It's Dorian's job to make sure you retain your arresting plum color, for it is exalted among the Hybridians. If you wish to use your safe word, now is the time to do so." Tristan surprised himself by offering the masc the means to excuse himself from the exhibition.

"Tristan, what are you doing?" Dorian demanded.

"My job," he replied through their psychic link. "Are you ready, Phoenix Ashe?"

"Y… Y… Yes. No need to s…safe word." Embarrassed by his stuttered reply, he reminded himself that he was a proud Elite masc. He lifted his head and took a deep breath, moaning at the ever-present cinfree.

As the attendants formed their lines and marched out to the parade route, Phoenix received an image of Tristan from the back, enabling him to follow his footsteps. He gasped when he realized Tristan was wearing the same body adornments as Dorian.

Wearing nothing but decorative chains and plugs, they strode onto Inaugural Promenade, where multicolored freesia shrubs lined the course, which had been covered with crushed cinnamon bark. The Hybridians' shouts and whistles were deafening as Phoenix and his attendants walked past the enthusiastic crowds. From the view Tristan was sending him, he could see their golden ornamentations were resplendent in the luminous afternoon sun.

With each step Tristan took, the anal plug nudged his pleasure gland, ensuring he maintained his erection. Tristan listened to Phoenix's thoughts as the young masc struggled to keep from begging for relief. His telepathic mewling was almost too much to endure. Phoenix was magnificent with his pure white tresses blowing in the breeze, his diamond-dusted, plum skin glistening and Tristan's aqua jewels sparkling in his cock and ass. The oval mask, which Tristan had commissioned to conceal Phoenix's features so no one would recognize his familiar client, completed his adornment. The gems outlining the gilded covering dazzled the admiring throngs lining the promenade. Phoenix Ashe didn't know it, but the aquamarine stones were exclusive to Tristan Faire. Their cool intensity matched his eyes, and everyone knew the significance of him choosing to adorn Phoenix in *his* color. He was publicly laying claim to the masc.

While they walked, the aromatics and the constant tugging on his sore nipples helped Phoenix to maintain his plum coloring. When they stopped for the applauding crowds, he had no opportunity to fade, because Dorian was there, prodding him with the heavy plug until he begged for relief. The Hybridians' cheering swelled each time he shouted out to the Divinity. Tristan sent him visions of the throngs' exuberance, but he was nearly incoherent with the need to come, making it impossible to focus on their adulation.

"You are amazing, Phoenix Ashe. Never have I been so proud to march in the display parade. Look how lovely you are. See how your cock has lengthened and thickened from Dorian's ministrations. Watch how prettily you beg. Your hunger for a climax reflects on me, and I could not be happier." Tristan craved the visions he transmitted as much as Phoenix, whose lusty responses kept his erection standing tall.

Tristan's proud smile stretched wide as his client's whimpers grew louder and his skin darkened even more from his praise. *Incredible!*

The parade began moving again until they arrived at the purlieu common. The marchers took their place next to the garland and cinfree-strewn pavilion. As if they all shared a psychic link, the participating mascs let out a collective moan as the strong fragrance floated on the breeze. The erotic scent of pre-ejaculate fluids mingled with the enticing aromatics, coaxing Tristan's cock to harden even more. He bit his tongue to keep from groaning out loud.

While they waited their turn on the stage, Dorian kept Phoenix primed on orgasm's edge with tugs to his nipple chain and nudges to the anal plug. The masc's powerful thighs quivered as he struggled with his need to come. They were certain to win the crowd's approval.

"Next up, Seminal Depository. Tristan Faire and Dorian Seaborn, attendants." The host's booming voice echoed through Tristan's thoughts. Tristan loved how the crowd quieted as he and Dorian made their way to center stage with Phoenix between them. Their pale lavender skin contrasted beautifully with his deep plum. His own rainbow braids swayed as he padded up the pavilion steps. His long, engorged cock shimmered with gold embellishments. Each step caused the filigree chains to tease his hairless ball sac. Tristan's pride in their grandeur rose as the eager audience cheered their ascension to center stage.

Shouts of "Tristan!" "Faire and Seaborn!" "Magnificent!" rang out as the throng waited for their display.

"You're up, Dorian," Tristan said, taking a step back so as not to draw attention away from his friend.

Dorian stepped forward, holding his arms out and greeting the assembly filling the common. He smiled and began rhythmically clapping his hands until the onlookers picked up the beat. Tristan swayed his hips, matching the movements to the pulsing applause. He undulated and teased, kneeling and grasping his ankles. Like he had earlier, he fucked the air, working the crowd into a frenzy.

"Listen to them, Tristan. They're loving it." Dorian's psychic communication interrupted Tristan's link with Phoenix. *"Do you think I could entice our masc enough that he turns black-orchid?"*

"I'm certain you can, and it would be spectacular. But Dorian, he's the mayor-to-be. I don't believe we should torture him beyond his endurance. He'd require relief and you know the pageant rules prohibit public coming."

"All right, you're the boss — this time. But I'm going to fuck his cock and force him to beg and scream. Be ready to support him if he needs it."

"Dorian, look at him, he's already vibrating with need."

"He'll be fine. Besides you're here to make sure he gets his mintage's worth from us. Right?"

Tristan didn't get a chance to reply before Dorian broke their psychic link. He watched helplessly as Dorian's efficient fingers removed the filigree threads holding Phoenix's cock upright. Once it was freed to sway with the heavy gold adornments, its lewd dance excited the crowd — and himself — even more. Dorian knelt before Phoenix and grasped the shaft in one hand while taking the penile jewel between his teeth. While Dorian fucked the magnificent cock with the wand, Tristan listened to Phoenix's appeals to stop and let him orgasm. The pleas made his own cock ache like never before, and without the restraining ring and wand, he would have shamed himself and orgasmed on stage.

Phoenix Ashe begged and shouted to the Divinity and when he could no longer stand the erotic stimulation, just as Dorian had promised — he screamed.

"Ibis!"

Tristan almost didn't hear the distressed shout over the cacophony in the common. When he saw his client's black-orchid flesh and his trembling legs, he pushed Dorian away and supported the towering masc until the tele-port he'd called for arrived. At his feet, Dorian Seaborn, holding the penile wand between his teeth, glared his displeasure.

"What the fuck is wrong with you?" he yelled through their connection.

"He *safe worded*, Dorian. Or were you so intent on revenge for his inadvertent insult to your overbearing ego, you didn't give two fucks? He's our *client* — a prestigious one, and you sought to harm him. Intentionally!" Tristan vibrated with rage, severing their psychic link and struggling to keep himself from strangling his friend.

"Don't you tire of them — those mighty Elitists — treating us like fodder beneath their oversized boots? Big feet, big cocks and big egos. The only time they venture into Hybridia is when they want their dicks sucked or to preserve their precious seed."

"I understand what you're saying, but Dorian, you chose this vocation. *I* choose to work as an attendant. We're good at what we do, and sometimes we happen upon the occasional reprehensible fool, but that doesn't give you license to torture someone, no matter how big a dick he is."

Once the tele-port arrived, Dorian surprised Tristan and helped him place their charge into the conveyance. Together, they carried Phoenix through the halls, ignoring the disapproving glances and whispered chastisements. *Apparently, word of our unsuccessful presentation has spread.*

"He will require relief once we get him back to his room," Tristan said.

"Well, *you* can do it. I'm done with servicing him. I'll not be his whore no matter what he believes." Dorian stomped out of Phoenix's room once he'd dropped him onto the bed, leaving Tristan to tend him on his own.

Tristan removed the gilded mask and other adornments, noting that Phoenix's skin tone had not yet begun to fade and neither had his erection. His lips were moving, and Tristan leaned over him to hear what he was trying to say.

"Ibis, ibis, ibis."

Hearing the agonized appeal brought tears to Tristan's eyes. His heart ached as he considered the best way to ease Phoenix's suffering. He called for a femme to bring him a healing libation and medicated ointment. Then he retrieved a towel dampened with cool water from the evacuation room. He bathed Phoenix while he waited for the drink and salve. Still the masc's coloring refused to fade. There was no other course—he'd have to provide him relief.

"Phoenix, I will help you. I'll give you what you need, but I fear it won't be pleasurable. Dorian has abused you and left you raw. The cock rings have badly bruised you. Same with your nipples."

"Ibis, ibis, ibis."

Tristan decided to wait for the requested items to arrive before beginning. Despite Phoenix's black-orchid hue, getting him to orgasm in his condition would take time. Dorian had tortured him long and well. Because of his notoriety, his friend was favored by the less reputable depositories, whose clientele enjoyed pain and suffering. He worked with them on occasion and had trouble compartmentalizing the two professions. He'd intentionally harmed Phoenix, an offense Tristan would never forgive.

Phoenix's anguished moan drew Tristan's attention, prompting him to pet the masc's arm and hair until he quieted. At last, the restoratives were brought to him. The femme who delivered them gasped upon seeing Phoenix. He refused to look at Tristan, but could not hide his condemnation from Tristan's developed telepathy.

"Thank you, Laughlin Ford. Your timeliness is much appreciated."

"You are welcome. If you need anything more, I'm here until the morrow." With one last glimpse at Phoenix, Laughlin shook his head and left.

"Okay, love. Let me assist you to sit while you drink this. It will help with your discomfort and speed up the healing. Then I'll take you into my mouth and give you the relief you require."

"Ibis. No more, *please.*"

"I'm sorry, love. I can't leave you like this. It's the only way."

"Ibis. You promised. Ibis stops all." A lone tear seeped from under Phoenix's lashes and trailed down his cheek.

His guilt threatened to choke him as Tristan swiped the droplet away with his thumb. He brushed Phoenix's hair from his face, then held the drink for him until he'd swallowed it all. It didn't take long for the soothing medicine to take effect, before Phoenix's tortured features relaxed.

With a longing gaze at his needy client, Tristan lay next to Phoenix and took his maltreated cock into his mouth. Even with his most tender ministrations, the future mayor cried. He tried to push Tristan away, from his bruised flesh, whimpering and repeating his safe words, but he was too weak to do more than pat Tristan's cheek.

"Oh, my darling. I wish this could be good for you. The Divinity willing, you can orgasm before too long."

But divine providence wasn't with them. Phoenix's inability to come frustrated Tristan because he couldn't give his client the relief he so desperately required. Finding the aloe ointment, he slathered a generous dollop on two fingers and worked them into Phoenix's anal channel. He located his pleasure gland, cringing because it had swelled — a result of Dorian battering it with the bulbous plug. He just hoped the analgesic would soon take effect.

Tristan massaged the gland, taking extra care to be gentle, as he spread the balm. Before long, Phoenix's whimpering entreaties to stop and leave him alone turned into blissful moans. Tristan sensed Phoenix wavering between enjoying the stimulation or allowing discomfort to control him. He sent the masc visuals of him fellating his tempting cock as he lapped the bead of pre-seminal fluid from its slit. He praised him through their psychic bond.

"Hmm. You taste delectable, like sweet grapes and honey. I could drink from your flesh for a lifetime and die happy." If only the Divinity would grant such a request. *"There you go, love. Let me know how good you feel. Give me your noises, your essence and your trust."* As Tristan imparted his thoughts, he continued massaging the pleasure gland, hoping the dual stimulation would trigger a much-needed orgasm.

"Need to come, please," Phoenix ground out as he gingerly fucked Tristan's mouth.

"Whenever you're ready, love. I can't wait for you to fill — "

Phoenix fisted his braids and fucked him hard, forcing the thick cock into his throat and coming. Around Tristan's fingers, Phoenix's anal walls spasmed as he filled Tristan with his spend. Phoenix's hoarse shout bounced off the walls as he came and came until he collapsed back onto the pillows and slept.

Tristan withdrew his fingers from Phoenix's body and wiped them on the towel he'd used earlier. He was tempted to swallow the masc's seed, but knew stealing an Elitist's fluids without their permission would get him fired. He spat them into the same wipe and discarded it before taking the aloe and applying it to Phoenix's bruised cock and nipples. Having done all he could for Phoenix Ashe, he drew a sheet over his sleeping form, noting his skin's mottling as it reverted to lavender.

Before he left the room, Tristan brushed a kiss against Phoenix's soft lips and picked up the chains and jewels that had decorated him. He'd just stepped into the hall to search out Dorian when the depository's director summoned him. With no way to avoid the dressing-down he anticipated, he first stopped at the compartment closets to retrieve his clothing and change. He removed his chains and other adornments, astonished that he was still wearing the plugs. Caring for Phoenix had so claimed his attention he hadn't noticed. He locked them away, making a mental note to clean and sanitize everything before going home. Regretting he'd not get to see Phoenix wearing his aquamarine jewels again, he locked them into the closet and set out to face his fate.

Chapter Five

Ninety-seven auroras had passed since Phoenix Ashe had made his inaugural deposit, yet he couldr.'t shake the notion he'd missed out on something life-altering. His days were much the same as they'd been before his visit to Hybridia. He drank his morning libations, viewed Segratia through his pristine windows and met with his parent at lunch. Still, that indefinable something that would make his existence worthwhile eluded him. Discontent seeped into his soul, leaving behind an unfamiliar aftertaste.

He'd awakened ninety-five mornings ago alone and bruised in a cold, cheerless room. He'd showered and waited for Tristan, but the attendant had never showed. Although the depository staff had provided his essentials, he had felt betrayed. Or was it deprived?

Phoenix had expected stage two of his visit to Hybridia would challenge him. He'd paid well to ensure his highly recommended paramour wouldn't be *too* easy on him. Phoenix faced a lifetime of giving orders and he'd longed for a week where he could just exist without the cumbersome burden of responsibility. Though it was difficult to admit, he had anticipated phase three with an eagerness that surprised him. He'd looked forward to the final component of his stay — an aspect that had promised contentment. *How long has it been since I've been content? Do I even remember the sensation?*

Then the refund had arrived, delivered by a messenger who'd refused to await a reply. Phoenix had read the missive, a quick impersonal apology from the director. They had given him a full mintage return and reassured him Dorian Seaborn was no longer in the depository's employment. No mention of Tristan Faire's fate, leaving Phoenix dissatisfied and curious.

Like he had several times since he'd left the depository, Phoenix planned to venture into Hybridia. He told himself his visits were to reconcile his personal feelings about the purlieu so he'd make a better mayor. It wouldn't do to let any residual animosity affect his governing.

He'd stood among the crowds during the last display parade, searching for Tristan. He'd sought out the golden ornaments and aquamarine stones, but hadn't spotted him. When Seminal Depository's representatives had taken to the stage, Phoenix had been left wondering what had befallen the mysterious attendant. He carried fleeting memories of hungry cerulean eyes and pale lavender skin and had a dim recollection of braids entangled in his fingers as he'd orgasmed into the most enticing mouth. The same mouth that had pressed against his as he had lain spent in his bed.

He touched his lips, trying in vain to recall the tender caress. He'd never been kissed. Mascs didn't share the intimacy. They fucked and fellated, but they never kissed. *I wonder why?* His parent didn't explain why, only emphasized mascs did not kiss—ever. He'd asked Gareth if he and his paramour in Hybridia shared such intimacies. The scathing sneer his friend had given him had made him regret his inquiry.

'We fuck and we suck. Why would I let him commit something so abhorrent?' To avoid further argument, Phoenix had been quick to agree with Gareth that swapping spittle was a disgusting practice. Still, Phoenix was curious about kissing. He secretly longed for the experience.

There was no parade today. Phoenix ignored the strange looks he received as he wandered the purlieu. It was a rare sight for the Hybridians to see a masc of his stature patrolling the side streets. They kept to the promenade or visited the seedier depositories. They didn't stalk the markets and hostels asking about a femme with eyes the shade of the Gemin seas and hair more colorful than the freesias growing in the common.

Frustrated over his inability to find Tristan, Phoenix walked among the cinfree-scented air, fighting the bile that rose in his throat whenever he sniffed the fragrance. It no longer affected him like it had. *I suppose trauma does that, strips something you once enjoyed from your character and leaves you empty and wanting.*

The only problem—he couldn't identify *what* he wanted. Tired of searching, he rested on an easy bench beneath a towering Staquotian oak. He closed his eyes and remembered the last time he'd dreamed of the femme who wouldn't leave him alone. *Where have you disappeared to, Tristan Faire?*

* * * *

Tristan Faire was a Hybridian celebrity, or at least he had been until the debacle of the solstice display parade. No one ever used a safe word during the public displays, and because the masc he'd presented had stopped their revelry as they'd carried him off stage, Tristan had lost his popularity. Yet, because he hailed from Hybridia and was femme, they kept his whereabouts from Phoenix.

From the market stall where he worked selling baubles, bangles and beads, Tristan watched Phoenix as he stopped and perused each booth. Sometimes he talked with the shopkeeper, other times he scanned the streets as if he'd lost someone. This was the masc's fourteenth venture into the purlieu since the twin solstice and though he could read his thoughts, Tristan had avoided the temptation to do so. Phoenix was entitled to his privacy and Tristan was ashamed that he hadn't done more to keep his client protected from the need to safe word. He blamed himself for the pain Phoenix had experienced at Dorian's hand.

The director had fired his onetime friend once talk of the incident on stage had reached him. He'd lectured Tristan, expressing his disappointment that their revered guest's visit hadn't turned out as promised. He'd refrained from dismissing Tristan, instead demoting him to an accompanying attendant. After thirty auroras, it had become clear his coworkers no longer trusted him. So, he had left the depository to work in his parents' shop.

Initially, he had been angry with Dorian and blamed him for his fall from favor. His self-pity had lasted less than a day before he'd taken responsibility. He'd been the lead attendant. Phoenix had contracted with the Seminal for him — not Dorian. Because of him, his client had been injured and he'd lost the chance to become a mentor. It was a bitter truth to live with. But what hurt the most was that the opportunity to proceed to phase three was forfeit. He'd looked forward to the bonding sessions since he'd first set eyes on Phoenix. The haughty masc hid a vulnerability beneath his arrogance that Tristan yearned to explore. Saddened at the missed opportunity, he turned to disappear into the stall's interior before Phoenix could spot him. He'd stepped into the cool shop when he caught a familiar voice as clear as if Phoenix were standing behind him.

"Where have you disappeared to, Tristan Faire?"

Tristan whipped around, expecting to see the tall masc, but no one was there, only the wares jingling in the afternoon breeze. The anguish Tristan heard in Phoenix tore at his heart, and when he looked for him he saw him still sitting on the easy bench. He hurried to close his little shop. Like an eagle drawn to the call of its life-mate, Tristan ignored his surroundings and answered Phoenix's summons.

"I understand you're seeking me out, love?" Tristan's forced bravado kept him from taking Phoenix into his arms and kissing him. It was what he wanted to do — to claim him and keep him. He also knew he would scandalize Phoenix with his exuberance.

"Tristan!" Phoenix's joyous expression rapidly changed to disappointment as he eyed him. "Wait. I've seen you before."

Tristan waited for him to recall when they'd first encountered one another. It didn't take long.

"On the Inaugural Promenade, and you *laughed* at me."

"Ah, love. I'm sorry you're disappointed. I'll just go."

"No! Wait. You surprised me that's all. It's that I had this picture in my head —"

"I know, darling." Tristan chuckled. "I put most of them in there."

"You're making fun of me again, aren't you?"

"No. Well, maybe just a little."

"I don't intimidate you at all, do I?"

"Oh, love. You scare the blond right out of my hair."

"I do?"

"You don't see any, do you?"

"Well no. But…wait a minute…none of the rainbow-haired femmes have blond in their locks."

"You're too smart for me. Come. Let's walk."

"Why not sit here and talk?"

"Because we're in the market, the depositories are beyond that and to your right, around the bend, lies the common. The aromatics are strong here, and I'd like to get to know you without the influence of erotic stimulants."

"The cinfree doesn't affect me like that. Not anymore…not since that day. If anything, it's a little nauseating."

"That settles it, we're walking."

Tristan sauntered away, expecting Phoenix to follow. When he caught up, he quickened his pace, eager to get the proud masc away from the effects of their environment. As they strolled through the streets, Tristan pointed out places he hoped might interest Phoenix. The library, the Chapel of The Divinity, the Center of Telepathic Expansion, the educational complex.

"That building there, the one with the broken-down play equipment and the weeds growing in the yard, it's where I went to school."

"That's terrible. Why isn't it maintained? Where are the children?"

"Femme education isn't in the mayor's budget. You don't see the descendants, because they're educated at home, so they'll have the opportunity to move out of Hybridia, but they live in poverty since the parent can't work full time if he's also teaching."

"But that's barbaric."

"It's either that, or do what so many others have done."

"What's the other choice?"

"Haven't you noticed, love? There are very few children. Most of the femmes can't pay the exorbitant storage fees of the depositories, not to mention the ransom of the incubation chambers."

"Then how do you procreate?"

"If they can afford it, a few will seek a hetero woman to incubate the child. But too often the result is tragic. The mothers are malnourished and the babe dies shortly thereafter, following a traumatizing emergence."

"But this means that before long—"

"We are declining in numbers, but we have longevity on our side. It's possible we're not yet doomed for extinction."

"But how? What can you do?"

Tristan gave him a small smile. "Who knows, Phoenix Ashe, something may come to us."

Phoenix didn't know what to say. How would he feel if he couldn't ensure his ancestry? Would he be as conciliatory? He wondered if there were anything he could do as mayor to help the Femmes. His childhood upbringing said no, while common decency said something else.

"Would you like to stop for a refreshment or nourishment?"

"Yes, please," Phoenix said, still distracted by his confused musings. Tristan had implanted the seed of an idea which needed time to take root and flourish.

Tristan smiled to himself as he listened to the masc's warring thoughts. Beneath Phoenix's arrogant exterior beat a soft and loving heart.

The libation emporium boasted refreshments, curatives and nourishments. Tristan led Phoenix to a corner booth, noticing the curious stares from the other femme customers. Tristan understood their inquisitiveness, since mascs rarely ventured this deep into the purlieu. He was certain the novelty of one of their own sharing a drink with a prestigious masc like Phoenix Ashe drew in more onlookers as word of their visit spread through their tele-links.

"Maybe this wasn't such a spectacular idea. I didn't think we would cause such a disturbance," Tristan said, as he began to hear snippets of the tele-chatter. His notoriety as a former attendant of Seminal always drew a bit of attention, but now the femmes wondered about Phoenix and whether he'd sought Tristan out for his sexual prowess.

"Why are they watching us?"

"They're curious. It's not often an Elitist will visit here," Tristan said, a quick scowl marring his otherwise flawless features.

"What's wrong?"

"Nothing. What would you like?"

"No, you're angry. Something's bothering you?"

"Let's go somewhere else. Someplace less crowded."

"Perhaps I should call for my transport and go back to Segratia."

"No! It's just that I didn't anticipate the attention we would attract. Come, I know somewhere quieter where we can visit and get to know one another."

They walked for several blocks without saying much. Phoenix asked about the men and women he saw huddled in the alleyways, often greeting Tristan, who responded with a smile or quick handshake. It took several of these interactions before Phoenix realized he'd handed them mintage with each greeting. *Beggars.*

"No, Phoenix Ashe. Did you hear a one of them ask me for anything? Or you? You do not get to come into my purlieu and disrespect its citizens, even if you're the next mayor."

"But they're heteros."

"Yes, they are."

"The Divinity says that heteros are abominations, a blight on Gemin."

"*My* Divinity teaches love and compassion for all the children and creatures of our planet. We are, after all, created in the Divinity's image."

"There's only one Divinity, Tristan."

"Exactly." Before they could continue their ecclesiastical debate, Tristan turned into a courtyard surrounded by pretty houses painted in varying pastel shades, reminiscent of freesia petals. The dwellings were small by masc standards, which were high-rises like Phoenix's home, or sprawling mansions, like his parent's. Tristan unlocked the aqua-tinted door to a quaint yellow cottage set in the far corner.

"You live here? I thought we were going to another establishment."

"Hybridia doesn't have but two, and the second is closed for a remodel. Please, come in."

Phoenix stepped across the threshold into the cool interior, taking in the furnishings. Overstuffed seashell-shaded divans strewn with aqua and seafoam pillows took up the living space. On one wall, a holo-screen displayed the Paradrae Sea, its gentle waves lapping the pink sandy beach at sunrise.

"That's one of my favorite spots in the prefecture. My parent would take me there for holidays when I was a child," Tristan said, unable to take his eyes from Phoenix.

"It looks quite peaceful. I've never visited. My parent was kept too busy with the incubation chambers and the responsibilities of tending his patients." At Tristan's puzzled expression, Phoenix added, "He is a physician. My time away from school was spent accompanying him on his rounds. 'Never miss an occasion to learn, Phoenix. Keep educating yourself,' he would say."

"Sounds like good advice."

"Of course. I would expect nothing less from my esteemed progenitor."

"Nor would I. Excuse me, and I'll fix our libations." Tristan disappeared into the tiny food preparation cubicle and left Phoenix to explore further.

The space was small but inviting, with fresh flowers set in nooks and carpets covering the floors. Before he could comment on the décor, the scents of sweetener and fruit diverted his attention.

"What is it that smells so delicious?"

"I made tarts this morning. Would you like one?"

"No, libations should be sufficient. Thank you."

Despite Phoenix's refusal, Tristan returned with a salver of tasty-looking pastries and a pitcher filled with a melon-orange liquid. The glasses he carried were tall and frosted. Tristan set the items on the rectangular table between the divans. He poured their drinks and handed one to Phoenix.

"Umm. This is delicious."

"Thank you. I make it myself from fresh fruits. It's made with the last of the summer melons. Are you certain you won't try a tart?"

Pastries were an indulgence Phoenix rarely saw. Rather than eating for pleasure, he consumed food for sustenance, a practice he'd learned from his parent. Unable to resist the aroma or Tristan's eager expression, he reached for one and took a bite. As the crisp flavor burst on his tongue, he widened his eyes, and his mouth watered. "Oh, my Divinity, this is so fucking good."

Tristan raised his eyebrows at the masc's vulgarity but thanked him, laughing to himself as Phoenix licked his fingers. He wished he could take a holopic of his esteemed guest. No one would believe the gorgeous future mayor of Segratia was sharing a repast in his living quarters. As much as he enjoyed having him in his home, he wondered why Phoenix had come searching for him.

"May I get you another?" Phoenix shook his head and finished his drink. As Tristan watched his visitor tapping a nervous tattoo against his glass, he asked, "Why have you been searching for me? What's brought you to Hybridia, love?"

"I was out for a walk and perusing the shops. You happened to see me, that's all," Phoenix said.

"Hmm. Do you recall the telepathic expansion center we passed earlier?" Phoenix nodded. "I mentioned that

I had attended, but what I didn't say was I graduated top of my class *and* no one has ever scored as high as on their T.A.E. as I have. At the time, I was but an adolescent."

"T.A.E.? What is that, exactly?"

"Telepathy and Awareness Exam. You see, the thing with psychic abilities, they only grow stronger as the telepath ages."

"What are you saying?"

"You can't lie to me, Phoenix Ashe. I knew of your presence in Hybridia as soon as you stepped from your transport, the same as I knew you sought me the other thirteen times you came into my purlieu," Tristan said, pinning Phoenix to the divan with a look. He was certain his intense scrutiny kept him from running away.

"Why not just look at my thoughts?" he asked, biting his lower lip.

"Is that what you want? For you to lose your private self to my psychic abilities?"

"I don't know. It might be easier —"

"Easier than what?" Phoenix met Tristan's questioning gaze and the hunger Tristan saw reflected in his dark eyes ripped a groan from his chest as he fought the inclination to read the masc's thoughts. "Tell me!"

Phoenix flushed, his skin darkening because Tristan's commanding tone excited him. He licked his lips and said, "I... I wanted to f...find out ab...about pha...phase three."

"Phase three of your contract with Seminal?"

Phoenix's hands trembled and he looked away from Tristan's piercing stare. He wondered if the femme was listening in on his thoughts. Did he hear how much Phoenix longed to know contentment? Could he read the unease which had sprouted in his soul since he'd reached his maturity? In that time, he had grown increasingly uneasy over his life's path and something told him that Tristan Faire was the key to his finding peace. To helping him accept his role in Segratia's political machine. To become more than a pampered Elitist. He'd come into Hybridia at every opportunity, seeking the femme who'd enraptured him since his visit to Seminal. He summoned the courage to admit his needs and trusted Tristan to take care of him.

"Y…yes." Shaking his head at his meek reply he tried again. "Yes! I want to experience all of phase three as promised. I wish to know contentment and I would like you as paramour."

Tristan's scowl gave Phoenix pause. He realized his mistake and said, "I'm sorry. I meant I would appreciate if you would be the *attendant*."

Chapter Six

Tristan couldn't believe what he was hearing. Phoenix wanted them to experience phase three of the depository's contract, the section where an intimacy often developed between client and attendant that bonded them through more than body. It was what he'd lamented losing when he'd left his employment. Now the masc was here, on his divan, asking for Tristan to show him what he had missed — what they had both lost.

Tristan had longed for the opportunity, but harbored doubts that he could achieve the desired results. Seminal had provided luxurious bonding rooms, complete with aromatics, sensual bathing pools and sustenance made from aphrodisiacs harvested from the outlying forests. Tristan had a small measure of the artifices used, but felt he brought nothing other than himself to the experience. His keen telepathic abilities would enlighten him as to Phoenix's thoughts, giving him an unfair advantage. He wavered over his initial inclination to say he would do it. He decided to give

Phoenix the choice. Deprived of the enhancements usually available to him, he'd require the masc to stay at his cottage with him.

"I would be honored to attend to you, but you must understand, without the benefits the depository offered at hand, I'm at a disadvantage."

"I don't care about the aromatics or the other femmes or the luxury."

"I'm glad, because with what I have in mind, none of those things are available. What is required on your part, is for you to stay here…with me. My living space is small, and there aren't many luxuries, except maybe fruit tarts."

Phoenix grinned and asked, "How long will I need to be here with you?"

"That's up to you, I suppose. The depository promised contentment and when the customer attained it, they were sent home. Seems cruel to me. During the bonding portion of their contract, the client and attendant achieve an intimacy that is unlike anything you can imagine."

"How so?"

"The clients are Elite mascs, like yourself, who haven't known much affection and communion. When such a connection is achieved, it's wondrous to behold—to know someone so well that you anticipate their needs and wants with a glance — to experience the ecstatic tears of their orgasm on your skin—to feel fulfillment from nothing more than a touch or a fleeting look." Tristan waited for Phoenix to digest all he'd said. He knew the mayor-to-be would return to Segratia and Tristan would go back to his lonely life. The heartbreak of Phoenix leaving would be worth any price for the experience. Tristan had paid it before, was still paying it. *Don't think about him, not now when you're about to get what you wanted, if only for a molecular hour.*

"I can commit to three auroras," Phoenix said.

"I need a week."

"I have obligations. Three is the most available to give you, but I can stay, beginning today."

"All right. I'll do the best I can with so little time, but I don't guarantee you will find what you are seeking. You realize, I don't have any clothes that will fit you. Do you want to go back to Segratia and pack a portmanteau?"

"I was under the impression clothing was optional."

"Well, yes. But that was at the depository and by the time we moved on to the third phase, we'd be comfortable with one another."

"I am comfortable with you, more than I thought possible being you mock me or tease whenever the opportunity is there. Now, shall I remove my clothes? And where should I set them?"

Tristan was taken aback by Phoenix's directness. After their last encounter, he hadn't expected him to exude such confidence. But then, he wouldn't be on track to govern Segratia if he didn't have such positive assurance. "Keep them on for the time being and let's just talk."

Tristan cleared the table of the pitcher and glasses, setting them in the food prep cubicle. He returned to the divan and sat in the corner, leaning against the plush arm and spreading his legs before him. He patted the space in front of him, for Phoenix to sit between his thighs, sensing the masc's hesitation despite his bravado.

Once Phoenix was seated with his legs stretched out over the divan's cushions, Tristan wrapped his arms around his massive chest and pulled Phoenix against him, smiling when he relaxed and rested his head on his shoulder. The soothing sound of the sea rolling onto the shore filled the room. Tristan didn't say anything but sent him a telepathic message to clear his mind and listen to the ocean, to their breathing and to their hearts beating. Tristan inhaled, the rise of his chest ghosting Phoenix's back. With each exhalation, his breath puffed on the diamond-dusted lavender cheek. He brushed the silky hair away from his face, sniffing it and memorizing the scent. The white locks were as soft and sensual as he'd imagined.

"Tell me about your childhood. What was it like growing up as the son of the prefecture's premier physician?"

"It was fine, I guess."

"Remember what I said about lying? Now try again, love."

"Lon...lonely. It was lonely. You see, my parent had the Aesculapian Board test my genetics for vocational predilection when I was four spans, and it was determined my genetic engineering was secured. I was destined for politics. After that my childhood consisted of holo-books, political theory, elocution and all the skills a politician might require. If I wasn't studying I was with the Arch Prelate, assimilating the Divinity's dogma. There was never time to play, to enjoy the benefits of my emergence, at least not until I left my parent's domicile. Then, I met other elitists at university and discovered comraderies. My friends Gareth and Temple showed me about being a masc."

"How did they do that?"

"They taught me about fucking, how to do it without causing your partner much pain, and how to suck cock."

Tristan had read Phoenix's thoughts before, about the friends he'd mentioned. He'd seen them fucking and fellating, and though the tableaux he had witnessed were erotic, he sensed the experiences hadn't satisfied the masc's soul. No, Phoenix needed more than to gratify his flesh to be happy.

Tristan brushed his lips against Phoenix's temple, noticing the small shudder that coursed through him. "You like that."

"Mmm. Yeah, feels nice. Makes me want more, but…"

"But? Tell me." Despite his demand, Phoenix hesitated. Tristan waited, rubbing small circles on his earlobe, feeling his appreciative murmurs against his chest. "You realize, I could just read your thoughts, but that doesn't promote the intimacy we're striving for. Share your doubts with me. What's wrong with wanting more?"

"Mascs, particularly Elitists, are raised to fuck or suck, kisses are considered abhorrent. It's something prohibitive in our culture."

"And you'd like to know about kissing?"

Phoenix nodded, his hair brushing against Tristan's cheek, causing him to shudder. He couldn't wait for them to share a bed. He kissed the masc's temple and murmured, "Come and I'll satisfy your curiosity." He waited for Phoenix to stand first, then he rose and clasped his hand, leading him into the bedchamber.

A holo-screen took up one wall, with the same scenes of the Paradrae Sea lapping the pristine beach. The tranquil *whooshing* sound of the water coming to shore added to the soothing scene and the room's ambiance. Like the living quarters, the bedroom was decorated in the same aquamarine and seafoam with the addition of pale yellow bedcoverings. Diaphanous fabrics swirled with pastels hung from the ceiling and when pulled together would enclose the bed in a world of its own. Sunlight filtered through the shades covering the windows.

Tristan removed his strapped sandals before stepping onto the plush cream carpets surrounding the bed. He knelt before Phoenix and helped him to remove his heavier shoes, setting them near the door. He stood, locking gazes with his guest. Phoenix's deep sable eyes reflected his own hunger for what Tristan was offering him. Tristan stepped forward, put his hand on Phoenix's nape and pulled him toward himself until their foreheads touched. *"Close your eyes and just breathe,"* he said. Tristan lowered his eyelids when he saw the white crescents of Phoenix's lashes lying against his violet cheeks. He inhaled and exhaled, relaxing with each breath, listening to the rhythmic sounds of the sea's waves rolling into shore. For several serene moments he was satisfied breathing in synchrony with Phoenix.

Tristan pressed his lips to Phoenix's, fighting the keen urge to devour the masc with his passion. *Seduction not domination.* He trailed the gentle kiss to the corner of Phoenix's mouth, teasing the tiny dimple which had beguiled him for a hundred auroras. From there, he left a trail of kisses across Phoenix's cheek, making his way to his earlobe, taking it between his teeth, not biting but fondling the sensitive flesh with his tongue. Beneath his hand, Tristan detected the masc's shuddering response. Phoenix hesitated before settling his hands upon

Tristan's shoulder. Encouraged by his response, Tristan cupped Phoenix's face and captured his lips. He smiled at the exaggerated pursing beneath his mouth. Phoenix's inexperience at kissing was evident, but his naïveté didn't deter Tristan. He tilted his head and claimed the lips he'd wanted to taste since he'd first seen Phoenix on the promenade. Phoenix was a quick study, opening his mouth to Tristan's questing tongue. Tristan languorously explored and enticed, licking and tangling with Phoenix's tongue.

With Tristan leading the way, Phoenix's quick mastery of kissing's finesse soon turned heated. Tristan's excitement climbed when Phoenix's lips softened and he stroked Tristan's tongue with his, sucking on it until Tristan groaned with anticipation. As Phoenix thrust his tongue into his mouth, Tristan felt Phoenix's confidence growing as he took his time to taste and probe. Tristan was surprised that his novice technique elicited such a passionate response from him.

Tristan moved them to the bed and drew Phoenix down to the mattress. Without breaking contact, he rolled himself onto his side and faced Phoenix. He stared at his flushed cheeks, heightened color and parted lips. Time ceased to matter. He spent what felt like hours memorizing the flavor and texture of the inimitable masc in his arms. His breath mingled with Phoenix's until they were breathing the same air and beating the same heart rhythm in a fervent tune of want and need.

Tristan broke away first, content to cradle Phoenix in his arms, to hold him and absorb his presence. Around him the masc's heady essence permeated the air, alleviating the need for cinfree. He needed no artifice to entice the tempting creature in his bed.

Phoenix was the seducer, awakening a need in Tristan he recognized as promising to be his undoing. Although the ancient divinities had warned of the perils of femmes loving mascs, it was too late to go back. Phoenix had ensnared Tristan's heart with his dimpled bravado.

"Tell me what you're thinking?" Tristan asked, running his fingers through the silken hair which had enthralled him since the afternoon he'd spotted him and Dorian walking toward him prior to the display parade.

"How very much my kind have missed because of their preposterous dictates against kissing."

"So, you enjoy it?"

"That's an understatement. I never thought my lips had a direct connection to my cock. I'm achingly hard right now and I can't decide if I want to kiss you again, or demand you fuck me."

"Hmm. How about if you just let me hold you?"

"But I only have three auroras. Shouldn't we do more…move along at a faster pace?"

"We will get there, I promise. Tell me about you going to university."

"It was much as you would expect. Classes, professors, after-class work. My subjects were very tedious. Not much excitement there."

"Is that what you wanted from school? Excitement?"

"At least something different. I'd been working toward becoming mayor and didn't socialize much, nor had I made friends. The other mascs shied away from me, thinking we couldn't possibly have anything in common."

"Sounds lonely."

"It was, but then I met Gareth and Temple. They were gregarious, bordering on outrageous, yet they respected my consequence. Except when we had too many fermented libations. Then I was just another playmate. Which I didn't mind, because without them, I'd only have had my hand for relief."

"I've heard the Elitist mascs are fond of the newest robo-courtesans. Didn't you own one?"

"Well, of course. But though the latest models are competent and their blow jobs passable, there's no emotion. Their mechanics, along with their apathy, are...depressing."

"So, Gareth and Temple, they make you happy?"

"I wouldn't say 'happy', but they're my friends, and I am content."

"Besides a good fuck, what are you looking for, Phoenix Ashe?"

"A phenomenal fuck."

"You're being flippant and I'm asking you a serious question. You've ventured into Hybridia fourteen times since we met. You must be searching for something besides a good fucking, because if that is all you're after, you could have found it in Segratia."

At Phoenix's silence, Tristan let the subject drop. Perhaps it was too soon for him to admit that he'd come searching for Tristan. His esteemed companion had been raised to believe he needed nothing more than his Elitist status and an acquaintance or two. He didn't know companionship or love. He hadn't yet realized Tristan was the one to give him what he was missing in his life.

"Come, let's take a bath."

"A bath? You mean in water?"

Tristan laughed at the wonder in Phoenix's voice. "Yes, in fine, effervescent Segratian water. No ion showers for us. We're roughing it."

Tristan rose and led Phoenix to a concealed chamber off the bedroom. The room belied the simplicity of the small house. Rather than a utilitarian evacuation room, the space was taken up with a giant tub, plush towels, shelves filled with lotions and scents. One corner was occupied by a chaise large enough for three. Outside the oversized window next to the tub was a primeval forest, rivaling the verdant landscapes viewable from his pinnacle apartment. When he spotted a crested ibis and an assortment of colorful birds, Phoenix realized Tristan kept an aviary. The sound of running water drew his attention away from the jungle-like scenery.

"Impressive," Phoenix said, turning toward his host and finding him naked.

"Thank you," Tristan replied. Phoenix raised one eyebrow and glanced at the towering trees. "Oh, you're talking about the garden. My mistake."

Phoenix grinned and tilted his head, studying the generously endowed femme. Beneath his perusal, the long cock thickened, and Phoenix licked his lips.

"Let me help you undress," Tristan said, taking Phoenix by the hand and seating him on the chaise. He went to one knee and removed his socks, then he stood and asked Phoenix to rise. He quickly opened his codpiece and rolled down his pantaloons. Next, he lifted the loose shirt over his head and tossed it with the other clothing in a pile on the floor. Tristan reached out and pulled on Phoenix's nipple ring. The gentle attention to the adornment elicited a groan he couldn't hold back.

"I believe our bath awaits," Tristan said, shutting off the water. Thousands of tiny bubbles rose to the surface, each one sparkling and reflecting the lights from above. Mesmerized, Phoenix stared at them, startling when Tristan slipped a restraining ring around the base of his cock.

"What's that for?"

"We're going to play, and I don't want to spend our time together cleaning out the tub. So, you'll wear a containment ring."

"What about you?"

"Darling, I was the premier attendant in all of Hybridia. Control is second nature to me." Phoenix arched an eyebrow and pursed his lips at Tristan's imperious tone. "But your eminence entices me like no other, so I'll wear one too." Tristan fastened an aquamarine ring around his half-erect cock. He stepped into the tub and took one of the fancy polymer bottles from a shelf, pouring a drop of the viscous liquid into the water. The scent of fresh pine and wildflowers filled the room. Phoenix joined him in the water and was surprised at its luxurious feel as the bubbles sizzled and popped over his skin.

Although the tub was large enough that they could sit side-by-side, Tristan sat in the center with his back against one end. He pulled Phoenix downward until he sat in front of him and Tristan could wrap his long legs around him.

He leaned his head against Tristan's shoulder and hummed in appreciation. "This is nice," he murmured. "I especially like the cushioned bottom and sides. The padding cradles you when you sit." Phoenix wriggled as he settled, causing the water to slosh back and forth.

"Shh. If you're very quiet, you can hear the birds singing in the aviary. Their song is quite unique and rarely heard in captivity."

"How is it that they sing for you?"

"I've replicated their natural habitat to the best of my ability. When you walk in, you can't tell if you're in the forests or my aviary. I'll show it to you on the morrow." While they spoke, Tristan massaged the stiffness from Phoenix's shoulders until he was completely relaxed against him. Sublime and drifting on a cloud of serenity, Phoenix shivered when Tristan spoke to him through his telepathic link. He hummed as Tristan rubbed small circles on his abdomen. *"What are you thinking?"*

"That I need to have one of these installed in my pinnacle."

"What? A tub?"

"Yes. It's invigorating and calming. Does that make sense?"

"The sparkling water is energizing. It's one of the qualities that makes Segratian aquatics so popular, especially in the outlying areas. The heated water's warmth seeps into your skin, your muscles loosen and bring you a sense of peace."

"How did I not know this?"

"Because you have been programmed to believe that all there is to your existence is the pursuit of your vocation. In your case it's your preselection as the next mayor. When have you ever had the opportunity to just breathe?"

Phoenix considered Tristan's words, realizing Tristan knew him better than Phoenix himself. It was unnerving and paradoxically comforting as well. He wasn't sure of his feelings over his revelation and changed the topic. "Tell me about you. All I know is that you are a paramour... I mean attendant for Seminal Depository."

"I'm not working there any longer. After the debacle in the common, I was demoted to a secondary attendant. After working in such a capacity for thirty auroras, I realized my coworkers no longer trusted me not to harm their clients, so I left."

"I'm sorry," Phoenix said, looking up into Tristan's eyes. Stunned at their tender expression, he glanced away. He was unaccustomed to affection.

"No, you have nothing to apologize for. It's me who owes you a big apology. I failed to keep you safe. I recognized Dorian was angry with you when he brought you to me before the display parade. I should have dismissed him, but I thought he was professional enough to let his anger go and give you the experiences you paid for. I can't express my regrets enough for the harm we caused you." Phoenix's dilemma confused him. He didn't know whether to forgive or to thank Tristan. Despite the pain he'd experienced, he had enjoyed the scene until they'd stood on the stage and he'd been forced to use his safe word. Phoenix wondered if Tristan sensed the remorse in him over Tristan leaving his job as an attendant. As the silence stretched out too long, he searched for something to say.

Tristan kissed him on the temple and began speaking.

"I was born in the outlying area. My mother was a surrogate for my two parents. Yes, I had two fathers, which I realize is different from the singular population of Prefecture Staquo. The three of them raised me in a small village where my mother and secondary father made a living, selling their wares. They were very artistic and free-thinking. I spent much of my time stringing beads for their bangles and baubles. I rarely wore clothes, because the forest is hot and humid, and the clothing was so restrictive. When it became clear that the Divinity had given me more than typical telepathic capabilities, I commuted to Hybridia with Mother to attend The Center. My parents opened a small booth in the market to sell the wares from home while I went to school. Once I was old enough to travel there on my own, my parents returned to the farming life they love so much.

"When I graduated, I accepted employment at Seminal Depository. The director stayed in touch with the dean for news of exceptional telepaths, and when he heard about me, he made me a very generous offer. It's how I've afforded my aviary, this tub, my cottage."

"Why would the depository want telepaths?"

"Are you really so naïve, love?" Tristan sent him a flash of the tableau he had used during Phoenix's inaugural deposit, that of Gareth, Temple and Phoenix fellating one another.

Tristan chuckled to himself at Phoenix's shocked gasp. "Oh. How could I be so obtuse?"

"My abilities helped to bring me the notoriety that attracted you to Seminal."

"I suppose, but it was my friend Gareth who recommended the depository to me. He said they had the best fellationists on Gemin. And from what I experienced, I would agree wholeheartedly."

"Thank you, darling. But we're only as good as the cock we're sucking. And you, love, are exquisite. Long, thick, essence like sweet grapes. I thank the Divinity for sending you to me."

Chapter Seven

Tristan lowered the lights, leaving the aviary illuminated. He'd had enough conversation and sensed Phoenix was ready for them to experience the intimacy he sought. When Phoenix questioned the lighting, Tristan hushed him. He adjusted the controls next to him to rewarm the water and rejuvenate the effervescence.

With his legs still wrapped around Phoenix, he held him secure in his arms, teasing the nipple rings and absorbing his needy moans. His own cock hardened at the sensual sounds emanating from him. Tristan ran his hands over the muscular stomach and noted that Phoenix's coloring had darkened. He nibbled the thick tendon in his neck, smiling as his eminent partner leaned his head to one side to give Tristan more access to his sensitive flesh. He couldn't resist the invitation and licked, sucked and bit until a trail of bruises decorated the flushed skin. Tugging the silver loops and indulging in Phoenix's lusty shouts, Tristan grinned while reading the turmoil of his thoughts.

More. No. Yes. Again. Stop. Fuck me. Damn this ring. Come. I must come. Please. Oh Divinity. Tristan!

It was time. Tristan straightened his legs, freeing the masc in his arms.

"Phoenix. Lean forward, love, on your hands and knees so I can prep you."

As if in a dream, Phoenix moved into position, surprised at his easy acquiescence. Grateful for the softness of the tub on his joints, he flushed, realizing that Tristan was staring at his naked backside. When Tristan touched him, he flinched.

"Careful, love. Don't want you injured before we get to the good part. I'm going to touch you again and ready you. See the pretty phalluses on the shelf? Choose one and hand it to me, please."

Phoenix glanced to his left, to what he had thought were bottles of scented oils. Upon closer inspection, he realized they were an assortment of gleaming polymer statuettes, each formed to the likeness of an engorged cock. There were long ones, thick ones and outrageously large ones. Many were textured, and a few were bulbous, much like the plug he had worn in the display parade. A particularly splendid phallus caught his attention. Its lovely shades of aquamarine and seafoam green reminded him of Tristan's eyes. When he selected it, he heard Tristan gasp behind him and wondered if he'd made an error. Should he have chosen something different? No, this was the right choice. He handed the phallus to Tristan and shivered at the arousal reflected in his gaze. He peered down and saw his cock — both their cocks — rock-hard and deep plum.

"Hands and knees, love." Phoenix hurried to do as requested, noting that the water level had gone down. "Don't want you drowning, do I?" Phoenix shook his head and shuddered when Tristan inserted a finger into his channel. He attempted to impale himself on the digit. "Do not move."

Tristan traced Phoenix's pucker with the smooth shaft, loving the way the wrinkled opening shied away from the cool polymer. He noticed Phoenix's legs trembling and said, "I'll use this to loosen you a bit. The phallus you've selected was made from a mold of my cock. I can't express how pleased I am that it's the one you have chosen."

Tristan applied lubricant to the anal stimulator and inserted it into Phoenix, groaning aloud when the masc began rocking and fucking himself with his endowment's replica. Fascinated, he watched it disappear and reappear with each motion. When Phoenix increased his tempo, Tristan removed it and set it on a shelf, grinning at Phoenix's disappointed whimpers.

"That's enough, love. You're ready for more. Turn around and face me."

Phoenix took a moment to catch his breath before following Tristan's directions. He sat and faced Tristan, taking in the femme's pale skin glistening in the diffused lighting. His eyes were huge, his pupils dilated and his cock—mouthwatering.

"Now, here is what we're going to do, love." Phoenix didn't glance upward, but continued ogling the weeping shaft. "Phoenix!"

He lifted his head and stared at Tristan, having forgotten he was there. The effervescent water swirled and grew warmer around them. Phoenix's passion was more intense than he realized. His skin was quickly darkening to plum.

"I don't know if I can tolerate much more teasing," he panted as he struggled to rein in his libido.

Tristan pressed a button near the shelf where he'd placed the phallus. The scents of pine and wildflower filled the air. The fragrances were known for their calming effects and within a few moments Phoenix's color was fading.

"Better, love?" Phoenix nodded, no longer experiencing the raging need to orgasm. "Now, what you do is sit yourself on my lap with your legs encircling my back."

"You're going to fuck me?"

"Not exactly. Do as I ask, and you'll find out what comes next."

Phoenix went to his knees and wrapped his arms around Tristan, scooting forward until he was aligned with the femme's rigid shaft. Tristan grasped him by the hips and guided him down onto the hard shaft in a slow, intimate embrace. His guttural moans echoed Tristan's. Phoenix fought the compulsion to plunge downward onto the steel heat of Tristan's cock, savoring Tristan holding him as he settled his legs around him. Against his body, Tristan trembled. Phoenix shuddered and groaned when Tristan bumped his pleasure gland. He fought the need to ride Tristan's erection as he steadied him with incredibly strong arms. Once Phoenix stopped moving and sat joined to Tristan's lithe body, he cupped Phoenix's cheeks and kissed him.

It didn't take long before Phoenix parted his lips and Tristan devoured his mouth, taking in his gasps and moans. His kisses were sustenance to Phoenix's hungry soul. Tristan pulled him closer, trapping his pulsing shaft between them. He held him tight, denying him the opportunity to move. Phoenix whimpered, trying for more friction against his throbbing cock.

"Shh. Listen and feel. I'll give you all you need. Trust me." Tristan's lips remained locked with Phoenix's and for a moment he wondered how he heard him. Then the femme's tongue demanded his attention and he surrendered to his entrancing heat, wrapping his hands in Tristan's braids and savoring the electric kiss.

"What are you feeling?" Tristan asked through their psychic bond.

"Excited, full, frustrated," Phoenix thought as he dueled with Tristan for control of their kiss.

"What do you need?"

"Relief."

"Besides that." Tristan chuckled and sucked on Phoenix's tongue until he whimpered.

"Touch me."

"I am *touching you, love. We're kissing. I'm buried sac deep within you. With your every breath your pleasure gland caresses my cockhead. Your nipple rings are pressed so tightly to me, I'm certain to have marks on the morrow. Your cock weeps between us, bathing our skin in your essence. I'm in your mind, reading your thoughts and sharing mine. How else can I touch you?"*

"I don't know. But I need *something."*

"Shh. You will get what you want. Have faith, love. Breathe and enjoy the experience. Pay attention to the water, taking heed of its effervescence as each bubble bursts on your skin and imparts its energy. Listen to the birds singing their songs of passion. Smell the intoxicating scents of the ancient

forest and absorb their sensuality. Notice how my heart beats in synchrony with yours. For now, we are one body and one mind." Eventually we will become one soul.

Phoenix mewled at the loss as Tristan withdrew from his thoughts. He broke their kiss and laid his head on Tristan's shoulder, burying his nose against his neck. He breathed in the femme's scent mingled with the forest aromatics and thought of what they had shared today, things he'd imparted to no other.

The effervescence on his skin drew his attention as he noted the tingling left behind after the sparkling droplets burst. Phoenix placed his hand over Tristan's chest and realized his heart's rhythm matched his own. Outside the window, the crested ibis' noisy call faded as the sun set. The songbirds quieted, roosting in their trees until the next aurora. Peace permeated his soul and he sighed his contentment. With Tristan's soft kiss against his temple, he closed his eyes and trusted him with his well-being.

Phoenix sensed Tristan listening in on his thoughts. He doubted he could find anything worth listening to. His thoughts were as silent as his body was satiated. He couldn't comprehend that his tumultuous mind was finally resting, nor that its tranquility signaled his acceptance of his intimate connection with Tristan. Against Tristan's abdomen, Phoenix's cock still exuded its precious essence, but he took no notice of its firmness. He inhaled, savoring the musky scent and the presence of Tristan's cock buried deep in his anal channel.

As Phoenix grew more and more sublime, he sank farther onto Tristan's shaft, pressing its head against his pleasure gland. He hummed and snuggled against

Tristan with each movement, hugging him even tighter.

"Look at me, Phoenix."

Phoenix lazily raised his eyelids and met eyes darker than the Paradrae Sea during a summer storm. Not shying away, he locked his gaze with Tristan's cerulean one.

Tristan could read every hungry desire on Phoenix's face just as if he were probing his mind. With infinite slowness, Tristan lifted Phoenix and set him down, using the water's buoyancy to ride his cock. Phoenix's small moans excited Tristan unlike any before him. Around his cock, the masc's ass quivered, its tiny pulsations warning of his impending climax.

As they grew in strength and frequency, Tristan clutched Phoenix to him and captured his mouth in a searing kiss, linking their thoughts and sharing their pleasure as their joint climaxes tore through their bodies. Simultaneous orgasms without ejaculation, the ultimate connection a femme could share with a masc. Tristan gave Phoenix a mental revelation of his satisfaction and drew fulfillment from his reflective response.

"Do you feel it, Phoenix Ashe? At this moment in time, we are one, heart, body and soul."

"Yes. What's happening? I'm coming, but yet I'm not. I don't understand."

"We call it the transcendence, the merging of psyches and flesh, a pure melding of the Divinity's chosen."

"Tristan, that was incredible. The pulsating sensations, I wished they could have gone on forever. You were everywhere, and when I shattered into one-hundred-million pieces of absolute pleasure, you brought me back down to Gemin and held me together."

"You were stunning. I couldn't stop watching you. Your eyes are nearly black, and your skin — black orchid. Do you see how wonderfully we contrast and how perfect we are for each other?" Tristan paused for Phoenix to respond, but when he remained quiet and introspective, Tristan chose to leave him alone to come to terms with what Tristan already knew. They belonged to one another and from this day forward no other would satisfy their souls.

Tristan lifted Phoenix off his still-hard cock and set him back into the water. He released a trace of the forest aromatics before refreshing the effervescence and stepping out of the tub. "I'm getting us something to drink. You stay here and relax for a bit, then I'll meet you in the bedroom."

Phoenix glanced at him and nodded. His glazed expression revealed how satisfied he was.

Unable to resist, Tristan kissed him on the nose before disappearing into the food-prep cubicle. He prepared fresh libations, adding a pinch of restorative herbs and liquid nutrients. They wouldn't eat again until the morrow, but the beverage would give them energy and stamina for the remainder of the evening.

He returned to his room, carrying their glasses on a silver salver made by his mother and given to him for his last emergence day celebration. Although his femme parents had marked the occasion sharing a fermented libation and nourishment with him, his emergence was extra special to him and his hetero mother. Whether they celebrated together or not, she always crafted him something from silver mined in the Outlying Mountains.

Tristan found Phoenix sitting in the center of the bed, lazily stroking his erect cock. The containing rings had done their jobs, keeping them both from spilling their seminal fluids. Phoenix's coloring had faded to violet in the time Tristan was preparing their refreshments, though he still wore a satiated expression.

Tristan set the tray on the stand near the bed and helped Phoenix to the mattress edge before he handed him a glass. He tried reading his mind and was pleased to note that silence reigned. The masc was blissful and at peace. Content. While they sipped their libations, they spoke of the day and about the two days they had spent together at Seminal Depository.

"Now that you are no longer employed, what are you doing?"

"I'm working for my parents at their adornments emporium in the market."

"After the position you held as an attendant, is shop-keeping satisfying for you?"

"I believe if you're good at what you do, whether it's selling baubles or fellating over-indulged mascs, you find satisfaction. I may not earn the mintage I used to, but I'm happy with my circumstance. I have shelter, nourishments and my aviary. I don't require more for contentment."

"I envy you. My life is filled with self-doubt. Certainly, I'm being groomed for the mayoral seat, but will I be a good mayor? I have a wonderful pinnacle apartment, servants to see to my needs, yet I am alone."

"I understand what you mean."

"You do?"

"My former status as a premier attendant gave me little time to make real friends. I thought Dorian and I were close, but he betrayed me by hurting you. After

I'd left Seminal, I realized I didn't have any friends, only coworkers."

"And I have Gareth and Temple. When I think about it, I can admit their friendship is superficial and conditional. If we're indulging in fermented libations and fucking, we're friends. But I could never express my doubts about becoming mayor without their ridicule. I once asked Gareth if he'd ever experienced kissing and the disgust he expressed made me wish I'd kept quiet."

"What does he have against kissing? Seems like he's missing out on one of the finest Divinity-given pleasures."

"After what we have shared, I agree."

Phoenix finished his drink and set the empty glass on the stand, surprised to notice his coloring had returned to its customary lavender hue despite his erection. He reached for Tristan's glass, the brush of their fingertips rekindling sparks of desire. He smiled at the beguiling femme, wondering if Tristan felt their intense attraction as much as he did. *What have you done to me, Tristan Faire?*

"The question you should ask is 'What am I going to do to you?' We have the night ahead of us. Come to me and allow me to take you to paradise," Tristan's seductive voice sounded through their psychic connection.

Phoenix turned toward Tristan and cupped his cheek, initiating their kiss. He'd had a taste of the oral intimacy and he wanted more. His traced Tristan's lips with his tongue, begging entry, and when the femme opened his mouth, he plunged his tongue into the wet heat and explored. Arousal, hot and demanding, gripped his cock, crying out for the constraining ring's removal. He clasped Tristan and rolled onto the mattress, lying so they faced each other. Tentatively he wrapped his hand around Tristan's cock, excited to see that it was as fevered and hard as his own. He circled the head with his thumb, coating the shaft with his pre-seminal fluid.

Tristan groaned aloud at the sensuous touch, content to allow Phoenix to set their pace. It had been too long since he'd been touched with inquisitive passion. As a femme attendant, he was expected to take charge. After his departure from Seminal, there hadn't been anyone to share his bed, except for Finn, a previous client who, after his Titanium package experience last year, continued to visit Tristan every seven auroras, but he never stayed the night. *Don't think of him. There's no point.*

He gave himself over to Phoenix's ministrations, sighing when he took his cock into his mouth and teased him without mercy. The masc's mouth was exceptional and when he bobbed his head, taking him into his throat, Tristan thought he might expire from the exquisite pleasure coursing through him. Every muscle in his body screamed for release, but with the constraining ring still in place, the all-consuming need to fuck overtook his usual good sense.

He flipped Phoenix onto his back and paid no heed to his astonished gasp. He kneeled between his muscular thighs and spread them. *"Raise your knees and hold your legs open for me. Show me your pucker,"* he commanded. Phoenix obeyed, holding his legs wide. His skin flushed as Tristan stared at his still puffy and dilated opening.

"Beautiful," Tristan said, circling the entrance to his sweet ass.

Phoenix's cry, eager and wanting, bounced off the walls while he tried in vain to get Tristan to enter him with his finger. Instead Tristan smiled and teased, watching the eminent masc fuck the air.

"You're gorgeous like this, Phoenix Ashe. Your muscles ripple each time I touch you. Your color is darkening and your pupils are dilated, begging me to claim your body and bring your needy self to orgasm like no other can. The way you look at me excites me more than all the mascs I've known. See what you've done to me."

Tristan stroked his cock, spreading his seminal fluids until the shaft was slick and shining with his essence. He fucked his hand and made certain Phoenix kept watching. The masc's legs trembled and his opening quivered. Without warning, Tristan plunged into Phoenix, relishing his cry of passion. He rarely felt this overwhelming need for another's body. Phoenix had awakened something in him that he didn't quite understand, but he feared the possessive emotions were love unleashed. He fucked Phoenix without mercy, pounding his flesh until the skin beneath him had turned black-orchid. He listened in on his thoughts, pleased that Phoenix's litany of "*Tristan, Tristan, Tristan*" was all that filled them.

Tristan locked into Phoenix's thoughts, sending him his impressions of what he was experiencing—heat, hunger, excitement beyond measure. "*Come, Phoenix Ashe. Let yourself go. Give me your pleasure and I promise, I'll put you back together. Join me, my love.*"

Tristan's orgasm roared through him as Phoenix's own climax squeezed his cock. The vice-like hold on his staff ensured he wouldn't leave the molten heat of Phoenix's channel. Tristan mashed their lips together in a claiming kiss while Phoenix continued coming. Each time Phoenix's climax ebbed, Tristan rocked into him once more, hitting his pleasure gland and triggering another. He lost count of the number and when he was sure the last one would be followed by unconsciousness, Tristan pulled out of his lover and left him lying in the bed sated. The soft expression on his passion-wetted face exceeded blissful.

Chapter Eight

Tristan returned with a warmed and moist towel to bathe an exhausted and well-used Phoenix. The sharp scent of their orgasms lingered, reminding his cock that it had not yet achieved satisfaction. Neither had Phoenix's. It was time to remedy that shortcoming. He removed his constraining ring and fought the urge to bring himself to satisfaction all over Phoenix's back.

Instead, he rubbed the cloth over the sated body on his sheets, marveling at the mottling of his flesh as it faded to its usual coloring. It was a rarity that he coaxed black-orchid to the surface of a masc's skin, but Phoenix Ashe was responsive like no one before him. While Tristan cleansed him and recalled the times his complexion had deepened so beautifully, he determined Phoenix's ultra-receptive nature was because his soul hungered as much as his body. That didn't deter Tristan, because he was more than capable of satisfying both.

Once Phoenix was clean and Tristan had wiped himself down, cooling his own heated flesh, he turned

Phoenix onto his stomach and lay on top of him, interlacing their fingers and stretching their arms overhead. He nudged his love's legs apart and rested his engorged cock in the cleft between his muscular ass. A shiver ran through him, much like it did every time he returned to his cottage after working. He had come home.

"Mmm. That was even better than the tub. Transcendence?"

"Yes. Multiple times. Exceeded all expectations. Are you…content?" Tristan asked, although he'd read Phoenix's mind and noted his usual tumultuous thoughts were quiet and his mind was as sated as the rest of him. Peaceful.

"I am happy and serene. Thank you, Tristan."

"You're welcome, my love."

With Phoenix lying beneath him, basking in his climatic afterglow, Tristan nudged his legs farther apart and breached him.

"Mmm. Feels good. So full."

Tristan didn't move, although his cock shouted for him to do so. He savored Phoenix's heat and, like he'd promised long ago, he wrapped himself in his curtain of white hair, relishing the sensuous cascade on his skin. In Phoenix's ear he whispered, "I love the way you smell, like the Outlying pines following a summer rain shower infused with our essence. It's intoxicating." Phoenix turned his head and smiled. As if it knew what he was talking about, his cock twitched, reminding him where it was and to get on with business.

He brushed Phoenix's hair aside and placed a chaste kiss on his favorite dimple, before starting a slow, torturous slide in and out. With each glide Phoenix's muscles clenched, holding Tristan captive. And Tristan was willing to be captured until morning's aurora bathed them in her awakening light. He'd known their union would be like this, soul-satisfying and impassioned. He moved faster, plunging in and out of Phoenix's well-used channel. He raised Phoenix onto his knees and clasped his shuddering frame tight against his. Femme and masc, making love as the Divinity foretold. Destined to be mated beneath the two-moon shining light.

"Hmmm. You're perfect, Phoenix Ashe. We fit together like we've been encased in the silky cocoon of the glasswing butterfly. In a way we have. Our transcendence ensures we'll be stronger and more beautiful than anything you have imagined. We will soar bonded in mind, body and soul."

With the imagery he'd painted implanted in Phoenix's mind, Tristan interlaced his fingers behind his partner's neck and turned his head, seeking a kiss. He held him by the throat and drank greedily from his lips. He released the containing ring and fisted Phoenix's cock, swallowing his heady cries. Slow and sure he pumped him until they were each frantic for the release he had denied them all day.

"Tristan. Divinity, so fucking good," Phoenix babbled with each stroke of his cock. Throbbing with the need to come and dripping with sweat, Tristan squeezed and tugged Phoenix's cock until he vibrated in his arms.

"Perfection," Tristan murmured, as he circled his thumb over Phoenix's cockhead, paying attention to his sensitive slit. His pre-seminal juices spilled over Tristan's hand and around his own cock, Phoenix's channel fluttered unceasingly as he approached his climax. "Close…so close. Feel what you've done to me. I shall love you forever, Phoenix Ashe. My heart and my destiny." With three more thrusts, bumping Phoenix's pleasure gland each time, Tristan's passion exploded. He spilled his seminal fluids into Phoenix's molten heat, sending him visions of their black-orchid and lavender-blush limbs intertwined in ecstasy.

"Tristan!" Phoenix shouted, as he came, shooting his ejaculate over Tristan's hand and into their hair.

Tristan collapsed with Phoenix beneath him, unable to move as his heart threatened to beat out of his chest. He rolled onto his side, spooning Phoenix, waiting for him to recover. Beside him he heard light snoring and realized his love had fallen asleep. He kissed his temple, pulled a sheet over them and soon he was dreaming of their future.

A few hours later, Tristan awoke with his cock hard again and begging to come. The rumpled sheet had been tossed aside and Phoenix was sucking him. As much as he wanted to lie back and enjoy the fellatio, he was too turned on to hold back his passion. Nearly a span had passed since he'd last enjoyed oral stimulation. Despite the numerous orgasms the night before, he was aching to come in Phoenix's talented mouth.

"Phoenix, love. You need to stop," he said through his psychic link as he moaned his pleasure.

"You're enjoying yourself. Let me do this for you," Phoenix answered back, redoubling his efforts and taking him into his throat until Tristan grasped his hair and pulled him off. Before he could explain he why he'd refused him, Tristan was surprised by a spit-wetted finger breaching him and rubbing his pleasure gland. He came all over Phoenix's flushed face with a shout, dousing him in his seminal fluids.

The stunned look Phoenix wore was priceless and Tristan had to laugh at the sight. Thick strands of warm ejaculate hung from his nose and hair like icicles from the roof tops. His skin had turned violet and his proud cock rose from a nest of white curls. His puffed lips begged for a kissing, so despite his fluid-covered skin, Tristan pulled him up to lie atop his body. He took his time tasting himself in the masc's tantalizing mouth.

"Come, let's shower, then I'll show you the aviary before we go eat."

Rather than use the tub, they bathed under an invigorating spray of effervescence. Tristan soaped Phoenix, cleansing his skin and stroking him to orgasm. He stared at the waste of sparkling fluids dripping down the shower's wall, wishing he'd had taken the opportunity to discover if Phoenix's essence tasted like sweet grapes. *What a wonderful start to the day.*

Once they had dried off, Tristan took Phoenix's hand and led him out into the aviary, not bothering with clothes. Tropical humidity and avian cacophony greeted their intrusion into the habitat.

"Welcome to my little piece of metropolitan nature."

"It's beautiful. The birds, oh my Divinity, there are so many. I can hear the crested ibis calling from the tree tops. How fortunate you are to listen to the Passeri song awaken you each aurora. The parrots...so colorful." The awe in Phoenix's voice as he stared up into the trees, identifying many of the winged beauties, captivated Tristan. He couldn't help but chuckle when Phoenix snapped his head around when something buzzed past his ear. "Was that a hummingbird?"

"Yes. One of three species I keep." Tristan strolled through the mock forest, keeping Phoenix's hand in his. They rounded a corner and in an alcove surrounded by ivy were several easy benches. They sat and enjoyed the morning songs with Phoenix asking about the fruit he saw sitting on a tray near several birdfeeders. "The citrus is for the butterflies. When they emerge from their cocoons, the aviary becomes a riotous symphony of color."

"I'd like to see that sometime."

"I would love to share it with you." Tristan met Phoenix's yearning gaze and smiled, promising to bring him to the aviary the next time the butterflies emerged from their chrysalises.

"Hello? Darling, are you in here?" A woman's musical voice called from the entrance, making Tristan wish he'd paid better attention to his telepathy. Otherwise, his mother would not have caught him and Phoenix sitting naked in the aviary. He should have realized she would come to see him when he sent her a missive that he was closing the shop for several days. Likely, his femme parents would not be far behind.

"I told you, we should have sent a message before barging in on him," Wiccan Tall, consort to Terra Gaia, admonished his wife. Tristan grinned, recalling the numerous disagreements his mother had had with her husband whenever he had visited them in his youth. They never agreed, but their love was undeniable. He was about to shout out his presence when he realized his parents had also entered the aviary.

"Do you see him?" Riley Faire asked.

"How can I, when you're half a cubit taller than I?" Loren Faire's indignant voice drifted through the trees.

"I'm so sorry about this, Phoenix. Forgive me," Tristan said, glancing at Phoenix with remorse and scanning the bushes for somewhere to hide.

"Who is it?"

"My parents — all of them."

"All of them? How many do you have?"

"Uhm, four."

"Four! Oh my Divinity!"

"There you are, darling," Terra greeted him as she rounded the bend, stopping short when she realized they were nude. "Oh my! I hate it when your secondary-father is right. I should have sent word we were on our way." His mother's high-spirited laughter brought the others sprinting to discover what was so hilarious.

Wiccan looked at Terra and said, "See, I *told* you we needed to let him know we were coming."

"Oh, love. Look at them. I believe they're the ones who have come — repeatedly."

Behind her, Riley and Loren chortled at their son's predicament. "It's nice to see you, son. But really, we didn't mean to see so *much* of you," Loren greeted him, glancing over at Phoenix and grinning.

"Leave him alone, love. Can't you see we've embarrassed him?" Riley rolled his eyes at his partner, placing one hand on his hip. "Oh, my mistake. Of course, you can see him. I mean we certainly see *all* of him."

"Mother, Father Tall, Parents Riley and Loren. May I present my guest, Phoenix Ashe from Segratia." Although he was nude, Tristan rose and kissed his mother and parents on the cheek. Phoenix also stood to his full six and a half cubits, smiled and shook hands with Tristan's family, who politely ignored his guest's clothing-deprived state.

"I'm going to fucking kill you, Tristan Faire," Tristan read Phoenix's thoughts. He glanced at his mother, noting her amused grin. It was obvious Phoenix had

forgotten he was in the company of very astute telepaths.

"Come now, Phoenix Ashe. Don't be embarrassed. We've all seen Tristan naked many times. And you should be proud of your stature and magnificence. Your beauty is unmatched, except by my own Wiccan Tall. Some would call your modesty a virtue, but we're not part of that group. Come, sit down and let's get acquainted."

Tristan sat back down and sent Phoenix a request to do the same. *"You may as well do as she asks. Mother can be very determined."*

"Yes, I can, my darlings."

"She also doesn't believe in anything resembling a private thought."

"The Divinity would not have gifted us with the ability to read minds if we weren't intended to use it. Isn't that right, Wiccan?"

"Yes, dear." Behind her Wiccan rolled his eyes and winked at Tristan before mouthing an apology.

"Tell us, son. How did you meet?" Riley said, as he sat in an easy bench and pulled Loren down to sit next to him

"Oh, do tell, Tris. If I'm not mistaken, this lovely masc is the future mayor of Segratia. Isn't that right?"

How does Loren know that? Tristan glanced at Phoenix to see how he was handling Loren outing his political status.

Next to Tristan, Phoenix squirmed and said, "Perhaps I should go and let you catch up with your family."

"No, love. Don't do that. We're really not so bad," Riley said, kissing his partner's knuckles as if that would prove his point to Phoenix.

"At least let me retrieve my clothing," Phoenix said.

"That sounds like a wonderful idea. I was showing Phoenix the aviary before going out to eat. Perhaps you all would like to join us?" Tristan asked, fearing Phoenix would leave before his three-day commitment to stay had ended. Despite the magical evening they'd spent, he needed more time for the masc to fall in love with him. Phoenix appeared confused over whether he should go, but Tristan counted on his good manners not to leave, and join the family for daybreak nourishment.

"Oh, drat! I was so enjoying the view," Loren said, staring pointedly at Phoenix, who jumped up and disappeared into the aviary's forest, looking for his way back to the entry.

"Oh, my Divinity. What a gorgeous ass," Terra remarked as he walked away.

"Mother!" Tristan shouted, sensing Phoenix's mortification before he left the aviary.

"Now, darling. Don't be a prude. You know we've always shared the same predilection for asses. It's why I married your secondary-father. He has a marvelous set of—"

"Terra, my assets are not open for discussion," Wiccan spoke up, his face reddening while he caressed her cheek.

"Oh, I don't know. Loren and I have often had lengthy discourses about your ass. He's of the mind that—"

"Riley, say no more or else!" Terra cautioned his parent through her telepathic link. Tristan also saw the gruesome depiction she sent Riley of what 'or else' would entail, making him shudder. Riley snapped his mouth closed and apologized to Wiccan, who had turned an enticing shade of pink.

"Heteros. Try as I might, I will never understand your kind," Loren said, shaking his head and grinning at a chastened Riley.

Tristan laughed at the old argument between his family members. His femme parents were of the opinion that his hetero mother and secondary-father were outdated in sexual matters, particularly when it pertained to femmes and mascs, while his mother and Wiccan thought Loren and Riley were outlandish to the point of embarrassment. Tristan realized they kept their opinions of Phoenix to themselves because, as their son, he was above reproach, an opinion he didn't share.

Tristan left his parents chatting in the aviary while he went searching for Phoenix. He found him dressed and seated in the living area. His worried appearance softened when Tristan walked into the room.

"Your parents seem…pleasant," Phoenix said.

Tristan's cheerful laughter rang out. "You're very kind to say so after what they put you through. But I do agree with one thing."

"What is that?"

"You do have a lovely, inviting ass."

Tristan watched, amused as Phoenix alternated between glaring and blushing. He could only assume the eminent masc was unused to such frank compliments.

"Let's go and eat."

"Yes, let's," Terra Gaia said from the doorway, with a trio of doting and smiling parents behind her.

Chapter Nine

The odd assortment of diners had just finished their meal and were chatting and sipping hot libations when Phoenix asked, "How is it that your mother is Terra Gaia and not Terra Tall, yet Riley and Loren carry the surname Faire, as do you?"

Before Tristan could formulate a reply, his mother supplied the answer. "Darling, Terra Tall? Really? Not only is it a dreadful alliteration, but look at me, I'm just a shade over five cubits. Terra Gaia is much more *me*. It roughly translates to 'Land Mother' and comes from the ancient writings."

"How can you question our surname? Do you not see us — Loren, Tristan and myself — we're fucking gorgeous!"

"I wasn't questioning the eponym's validity, but rather asking why Terra hadn't taken Wiccan's name. I didn't intend to offend you. Please accept my apologies."

"My parents are teasing you, love. Riley and Loren are dreadful tricksters, which is why they don't come down from the Outlying area too often. Last time they visited, they barely dodged being arrested for cock racing."

"Oh, puhleez!" Loren said, waving his hand as if he were chasing away a pesky insect. "The tavern sign clearly read, 'Cock races held at sunset.' We were on time with our birds in a cage. When we found out they meant *cocks* rather than feathered two-legged cocks, we removed our pantaloons and happily challenged all comers."

"There were quite a few comers, if I recall," quipped Riley.

"It was a *disaster*," said Tristan. "The roosters got loose, and between a tavern full of femmes jacking their appendages competing for the fastest orgasm and the feathers flying, it was like a bad tableau from a porn-horror vision."

"When Wiccan arrived to corral the wayward cocks — the birds, not Tristan's parents — Loren and Riley were arguing with the constable that it was an honest mistake anyone could have made," Terra said, shaking her head at their antics.

"Well, to be truthful, you must possess suitable equipment," Loren said with a wink and grin. "Riley and I have the right stuff."

Unable to hold his mirth in any longer, Phoenix broke into hearty laughter, imagining the wild scene they described. In Segratia, he'd have been humiliated to have called attention to himself in such a way, but the usual social mores didn't apply in Hybridia. He found the unconventional ways very liberating.

Faster than a pinwheel blowing in the wind, Terra directed the conversation toward his real life.

"Tell me, Phoenix. What is it you want to accomplish during your tenure as Segratia's mayor?"

"I haven't given it much consideration, although I'd be happy just to maintain the status quo."

"How forward thinking of you." Sarcasm dripped from Terra's tone. Next to her, Tristan cringed.

"Terra, leave him alone," Wiccan chided. "At least he's not making any sweeping changes that will bring any more fallout onto our kind."

"What do you mean 'fallout'?" Phoenix asked, drawing his eyebrows together. He didn't understand what he'd said to earn Terra's animosity and hoped Wiccan or Tristan could enlighten him.

"Have you been living in a bubble?" Terra demanded. "Don't you see what's happening to the heteros of Gemin?"

"I must admit, my upbringing and residence in Segratia is rather insular. What am I missing?"

"Phoenix, much of the prefecture treat my mother and Wiccan as third-class citizens. The hierarchy in our world is grossly unfair."

"How so?"

"Our populace's potential is classified and stymied based on whether they are emerged as hetero, masc or femme. Heteros learn from childhood their destiny is to serve the mascs either as servants or menial laborers. To seek another way, they leave the cities to fend in the Outlying area, living on farms without a means to educate their children or care for their elderly. Medical assistance is exorbitant and rarely offered in the wilds. Unlike the femmes, they can procreate, so they're in no danger of extinction, but their lot in life is limited." Wiccan's simplified explanation satisfied Phoenix's curiosity and gave him something to contemplate. He had never considered the effect the caste system had on the populace. It was just how things were.

"I am surprised by your ignorance," Terra said, surprising him with her frankness. "The discriminatory practice has been in place for a thousand spans. Do you shut your eyes to the plight of our people whenever you venture into Hybridia? We live in the streets, because even if we had the means, Staquo law forbids us to own property."

"I can understand your frustration, but who am I to tamper with the status quo?"

"You are the next mayor of Segratia. And if change can't begin with you, then who will take up our cause?"

"Perhaps we've overwhelmed or maybe overestimated Tristan's friend," Riley said, with disappointment written across his face.

"Have a little faith, love. I do," Loren said, taking Riley's hand in his and interlacing their fingers.

"What about the femmes?" Terra demanded. "If he won't stand up for the heteros, what about you, and Riley and Tristan? Your kind are dying off and nobody seems to give two fucks."

"But Tristan told me —"

"What? That everything would be fine because he has longevity on his side and something will come to him? Those are the same platitudes the femme leaders have spouted for the last one hundred spans. Meanwhile, their populations are diminishing at an appalling rate."

"Mother, please."

"Please what? Hold back? Keep my mouth shut while I watch my son's people fade away? Not only are the old laws killing you off, they are relegating your station to little more than that of a whore!"

"Mother!" "Terra!" "What?" Phoenix noticed that all around the busy establishment, eavesdroppers gasped and watched them. He was appalled at the way Terra Gaia spoke to her son. Tristan may have been an attendant for the seminal depositories, but from what he understood the Hybridia populace revered the attendants. Phoenix imagined that listening to someone speaking harshly to one of their own was tantamount to criticizing them all.

"Damned heteros, thinking they were better than the attendant femmes," Phoenix heard one angry femme mumble.

"Mother, you go too far! I love you, but until you apologize to myself and Phoenix, I'm banning you from my circle," Tristan said, squeezing Phoenix's arm.

Certain that the crowded diner patrons were listening to their discourse, Phoenix was torn over whether to comfort Tristan or leave at once for Segratia. He didn't like conflict and this family dispute made him uncomfortable.

"Terra, you must say you're sorry," Riley and Loren begged.

Loren added, "We know you're not happy with our son's chosen profession, but for you to display your vehemence in public toward Tris is not to be tolerated."

"My love? Don't be so stubborn that you refuse to take back your words. Tris is your heart, and I know you. If you hurt him, you hurt yourself. I hate to see you—both of you—in pain." Wiccan squeezed his wife's shoulder, but she pulled away from his touch.

"Tristan? What does banning from your circle mean?" Phoenix wanted to know, noting Tristan's welling tears.

"Until she says she is sorry, all communication with her is severed. This includes not only physical, but also psychic contact. From this point, I banish Mother from my thoughts, your thoughts and those of my femme parents. She will not spy on me, nor any of my acquaintances. If she apologizes, I'll bring her to you where Terra Gaia will, with due respect for your station, make her amends."

"Don't you think you are being a little harsh?" Riley asked. "She is your mother and, as always, concerned for your welfare."

"Did you not hear her? She called me a whore!"

"That was uncalled for, love. I'm with Tris on this on, and will abide by his ban," Loren said. He turned to Terra, who looked stricken with what she'd brought on herself. "I'm sorry, Terra. I am breaking our connection until I hear from Tris."

Phoenix shook his head as Tristan's mother rolled her eyes. He hoped her obstinance wouldn't keep her from making amends. From the high emotions swirling around him, he suspected would be quite a while before her remorse took hold.

Studying his partner, Riley sighed and nodded. "Terra, don't take too long to reconcile with our boy, for I shall sorely miss you poking around in my thoughts. I too will follow his directive, for now."

"Tris… I accept your edict, but as Terra's husband I cannot in good conscience sever our bond. However, I promise you I will keep your privacy until she apologizes to you and Phoenix."

"Thank you, Wiccan. I recognize what I have asked of you all has put you in a difficult position. I appreciate your support."

Wiccan nodded and helped Terra rise, escorting his mutinous spouse from the establishment.

With a last look at his mother, Tristan sent her a final message, reassuring her of his love and saying he looked forward to hearing from her. Eerie silence met him as she ignored his missive. He turned to his parents and Phoenix, apologizing for ruining their pleasant interlude.

"Don't be ridiculous. Terra will reexamine all she said, and what led up to her behavior. She'll see the error of her ways. Then, she may have to concoct a reasonable excuse for her inexcusable comment, before she works up the courage to come speak with you again," Riley said.

Tristan recognized his parent's words were meant to console him, but they did little to lessen his anger. This time Terra had gone too far.

"Oh, absolutely. I say shouldn't be more than a span...two at the most for her to retract her insult," Loren added.

Incredulous, Phoenix asked, "It will take your mother *two* spans to apologize? Seems like an inordinate amount of time for a simple 'I'm sorry.' Is she really so obstinate?"

"Well, yes. She's Terra. It's what she does. But, on the bright side, familial conflict always energizes her. Wiccan will reap the conjugal benefits," Riley said with a lewd wink.

"Oh, my. I hadn't thought of that. He'll be insufferable, walking around all day, grinning like a fool. But the work she puts out *will* make us a tidy sum."

"There is that," Riley agreed with Loren. "We'll soon have extra mintage coming our way."

"What do you mean?" Tristan wanted to know.

"When she's stewing, your mother creates the most incredible silver pieces. You remember the tray you love so much?"

"Yes? It's there on my table at home."

"It's a product of one of her and Wiccan's disagreements. I recall it was over her putting turnips into the gravy."

"Wiccan *hates* turnips."

"Wouldn't she know that?" Phoenix asked, glancing from one to another. "Perhaps she wanted to provoke their disagreement."

"Well, of course she did. That woman is a sex nymph," Loren said.

"Your assessment of our darling Terra is quite astute," Riley stated with a grin.

"Enough! This is my *mother* you're talking about."

"Just don't tell her we know her little secret. The point is, when she's stewing, she creates and the shop profits," Riley said, sitting back in his chair and signaling the server for libation refills. Now that the confrontation had ended, the other diners went about their business, a few patting Tristan's shoulders in silent support and others sending him encouraging messages.

Tristan was glad that Riley and Loren settled in to visit with him and Phoenix. He hadn't seen them since the cock debacle in the tavern, and was eager for them to become acquainted with Phoenix.

"I've missed you two. Tell me how is the farm?"

"Well you know, much the same as always. Animals, planting, harvesting and when there's time—crafting for Bangles and Sterling. Loren started a new project and the place is a mess."

Phoenix raised his eyebrows and listened, intrigued, as Riley explained the crafts were for the shop he and Loren owned and contracted with Terra for silver pieces.

"Another painting?" Tristan asked.

"You know me too well, love. I'm doing a study in cerulean for the next equinox display."

"That sounds intriguing," Phoenix said. "Maybe Tristan should model for you. His eyes most assuredly are worth studying."

"Oh, puhleez," Tristan said, sounding just like his parent. "I've done my share of sitting for his artistic endeavors."

"That's true, but perhaps since you are no longer with the depository, you can make time for an impressionist canvas I'm considering painting."

"I'll think about it."

"Speaking of the depository, will you go back to working as an attendant?" Riley asked. Loren set down his drink and focused on Tristan while Phoenix listened intently.

"Perhaps. The mintage was certainly generous, and I enjoyed the work."

Phoenix heard Tristan's parents tittering, realizing they were adolescents at heart.

"Stop it, you two," Tristan scolded. "The job isn't about the attendant and his pleasure, but making sure the client receives the optimum enjoyment for their mintage. I appreciated their satisfaction even if it meant I went without relief for several days. I was exceptional at my profession, and if Phoenix hadn't been abused by Dorian, I'd still be happily employed."

"Oh, my dear. We're so sorry that Dorian hurt you. Our Tris is right. He was a great attendant and please don't judge him from one bad experience," Loren said.

"I wasn't aware my encounter with Seminal was common knowledge. They assured me of privacy."

"This is Hybridia! The display parade is not to be missed. Loren and I were in the crowd that afternoon. I must say, darling, you were absolutely resplendent on stage," Riley gushed.

"Oh, yes! You were *magnificent*. We were a bit disappointed you had to safe word. But when Tris explained how Dorian was abusing you, we wanted to banish him from the prefecture."

"You're embarrassing Phoenix," Tristan said, hoping they'd take their attention off his display parade appearance.

"You were the most attractive of the participants —"

Tristan turned at Phoenix's horrified sounding gasp.

"Rest assured, love. You were well-masked so other than my parents, no one was privy to your identity," Tristan said, patting Phoenix's hand.

"Tell me though, what brought you to the display parade? Mascs of your stature aren't generally quite...shall I say 'visible.' They come to the depositories, leave their fluids and return home. Rarely do they take part in the stage exhibitions put on for Hybridian entertainment," Riley said.

Phoenix hesitated, uncertain if he wanted to share something that was private with these femmes he'd just met. Tristan's encouraging smile removed any lingering anxiety, and he said, "I was born during the twin solstice, and chose to make my inaugural deposit during their zenith, which according to the old prophecies would ensure my offspring's singular purity."

Riley and Loren studied him until he squirmed. They didn't express outright disapproval, but their expressions were little more than tolerant. Phoenix wondered what he had said now to erase the easy camaraderie they were sharing. He looked to Tristan for an explanation and found that he also wore his parents' same disapproving scowl.

"What have I said to offend you? I don't understand?"

Riley spoke up first. "Do you not hear yourself, love? When you use words like 'singular purity', it's demeaning to those of us who are deemed impure by the masc population."

"But you are. You're femmes. The Divinity tells us that the mascs will inherit Gemin. It's why we were the ones chosen to rule and keep the laws. It's why it's paramount that our singular purity remains intact."

"Oh, love. I understand that is what you were *taught* to believe. But consider this—how did the Divinity spread the word of your singular greatness?"

"It's recorded in the old media," Phoenix replied.

"And who recorded these antiquated laws?

"Why, the Divinity's chosen—the pure singular mascs."

"And why do you think that was?" Tristan queried.

"Because they were *chosen!*"

"And who said they were chosen?"

"The mascs who recorded the ancient words."

"Exactly," Loren, Riley and Tristan said in unison.

Phoenix glanced from one to another, wondering why they looked so smug. Loren was leaning back in his chair with one eyebrow raised, as if he were waiting for something from him. *Do they enjoy keeping him off guard? And why isn't Tristan saying anything? How is it possible that he believes the drivel they're spouting?* The doctrine his Arch Prelate had taught him stated in no uncertain terms that mascs were the chosen. How could these femmes' beliefs contrast so widely from his own?

Despite the unexpected visit and the way Tristan's family had suspended their interlude, he was rather satisfied, physically if not emotionally.

"Tristan, I believe I shall return to Segratia."

"But, we haven't finished with all you wanted to accomplish."

"I don't know what I was thinking. I really can't afford to stay here any longer. There is so much left to do before my inauguration. I do thank you for your hospitality. Loren, Riley, it was a pleasure to meet you. Your philosophies are…intriguing and I shall consider what you are saying."

"Phoenix love, I hope we haven't done anything to chase you off," Riley said. "We can get carried away when it comes to religion and politics and, in my case, art."

"I always forget how formal the Segratians speak. It's rather unique," Loren added, looking none too concerned over Phoenix's hasty departure.

"No, Riley, I admire your passion. There are many waiting for me to finalize my ascension. I do hope we can meet again," Phoenix said as he rose from the table. He gave them a smile and walked to the door, ignoring the stares of the other patrons.

"I wish you would reconsider staying," Tristan said, standing next to him. He followed him out onto the sidewalk holding on to his arm. "After experiencing transcendence…the couple…well, there's just more to it than sex."

"Tristan, it was a splendid night and one I shall never forget, but I'm about to become mayor and I have priorities which must be attended to. Thank you for the morning nourishment and libations. I hope to see you at my inauguration." With a quick kiss to Tristan's cheek, Phoenix hailed a passing transport and returned to Segratia, ignoring the troublesome pang somewhere near his heart.

Chapter Ten

Ten auroras had come and gone since Phoenix had left Tristan sitting in an establishment drinking morning libations with Riley and Loren. Guilt accompanied him for about twenty milli-minutes before anger took over. How dare the femmes and Terra Gaia make him question everything he had believed since his emergence? He was a singular masc, fated by the Divinity's word to become the next Segratian mayor. His lot was destined and his superiority secure.

Yet doubt niggled his conscience and he struggled to pluck out the seeds of dissension which had taken root. He spent time in the Temple of the Divinity, seeking answers which never came. He could not find the words within the sacred records, or fragile texts which confirmed femmes and heteros were abominations. Why then were they considered inferior? Was Tristan right? Had the Divinity created all of Gemin's populace from her image? If so, that meant femmes, mascs and heteros should live together in harmony, as the

Divinity directed. *Abide in peace and tranquility in my name.* The old scripture occupied Phoenix's thoughts every day. At night, the words kept him from a restful sleep.

He'd met his friends Gareth and Temple once since his return. They'd spent the evening indulging in potent Segratian fermentations until they were too inebriated to do more than lie on the divans like beached narwhals on a sandy Paradrae beach.

"Do you ever wonder if the teachings from Temple were wrong?"

"Wha? I swear I never said a word," Temple protested from his end of the divan before he stood and staggered to the evacuation room.

"Not you, you crazy bastard. I meant the Divinity's Temple!" Phoenix shouted.

"What the fuck's wrong with you? You've been acting strange ever since you came back from Hybridia. What happened, you couldn't *rise* to the occasion?" Gareth snickered at his little joke, then followed it with a rude belch before refilling his snifter. "Want s'more?" he asked, raising the near-empty bottle of aqua liquid.

"No, thank you. I've had plenty," replied Phoenix, thinking the libation's color resembled Tristan's beguiling eyes. The puzzled hurt in the femme's beguiling blue eyes had haunted him since he'd left Tristan sitting in the establishment with his parents. "I met others in Hybridia, femmes and heteros, who have caused me to question the beliefs we were raised with."

"What's to question? There is a Divinity. We worship. We pay tithes. The rest is veneer and distraction which serves to disguise the fact we're lining the pockets of a greedy overweight pontificator."

"Are we talking about Jessup Windraptor?" Temple asked, walking into the room and straightening his codpiece. "The old goat wanted me to blow him when I served the Divinity during Equinox services twenty spans ago."

"That's disgusting. What did you do?" Phoenix asked, recalling his own imperiled encounter with the lascivious old masc.

"Told my parent what the lecher wanted. He marched to Temple, unmindful that Jessup was a man of Divinity, and punched him, threatening to expose his sick proclivities to the Arch Prelate and Segratian populace. Never been so proud of my parent as I was on that day," Temple said, with a tear rolling down his cheek.

Phoenix shuddered, recalling how different his experience had been when he'd tried to tell his parent of the perversions forced upon him by Prelate Windraptor. The esteemed physician had lectured him about his duty as one of the chosen to serve the whims of the Divinity's representative without complaint. It wasn't long after Temple's parent had confronted Jessup that he'd left Segratia, but by then Phoenix had been subjected to his abuses for half a span.

"You know I've been reading a few of the old scriptures, and I can't find anything specific denouncing femmes or heteros. Why then do we?"

"Give it a rest, Ashe. Are we going to fuck or what? If not, I'm grabbing another bottle of your exceptional ferment."

"You two play. I've imbibed too much, so I'll observe," Phoenix said, disappointed in his friend's over-occupation with his cock. He hadn't indulged in sex since leaving Hybridia and even spending the night observing Temple and Gareth fucking and fellating didn't excite him. He'd experienced more provocative nights reliving his and Tristan's transcendence. He leaned back against the divan's plush cushions and watched as his friends quickly stripped.

Despite the fermentations they'd consumed, it didn't take long for their cocks to stir. They positioned themselves face to groin and fellated one another with sloppy precision. Before long, amid noisy groaning and moaning, they were fucking each other with their fingers. They rolled and writhed on Phoenix's carpet, trying to make the other orgasm first. *They'll be doing that for hours with as much distillation they have consumed.*

Bored with his friends, Phoenix closed his eyes and thought of Tristan. What was he doing? Had he gone back to working at the depository? He wondered if Terra had been forgiven yet, but then remembered Tristan had promised to bring her to see him once she'd made her amends. He'd thought about going to see Tristan, ask him to fuck him one more time, so he could drive the femme from his thoughts. He craved transcendence and feared he'd never again know its rapture.

Come to me, love. I'll give you what you need...what we both need.

"Get out of my head!" Phoenix shouted, tossing his glass against the wall, shattering it.

"Phoenix? What the fuck?" Gareth mumbled around a mouthful of cock.

"Sorry, guys. I'm calling it a night. If you need anything the robo-serv will take care of you." The mechanical device had emerged from its niche within seconds of Phoenix's glass hitting the wall and was cleaning up the glass shards.

C.L. Etta

"Aww. Don't go, Phoenix. You can fuck me while Gareth sucks me off."

"Sounds delightful, but no thanks. I have a lot to consider before inauguration day. Have a good time." Phoenix didn't expect a reply, since Gareth and Temple were preoccupied before he'd left the room. Their sucking noises faded away as Phoenix approached his sleeping quarters. He was left alone with salacious images of himself and Tristan filling his thoughts.

He wasn't certain, but he thought Tristan was sending him visions of their transcendent night together. How else could he account for the brilliant images that haunted him night and day? Visions of him coming more often and harder than he ever believed possible. Tristan's face frozen in ecstasy as he ejaculated in Phoenix's spasming channel. Phoenix begging the femme to keep fucking him. *What enchantment has Tristan cast upon me?*

Kissing. Divinity, he missed the intimate caress. He'd tried touching Temple's lips with his earlier tonight, but his friend had turned away, glaring at Phoenix as if he were depraved. Perhaps he was. Mascs never kissed and Phoenix had always been the consummate masc.

Stop torturing yourself...both of us. Come to me.

"Tristan, are you there, or am I imagining your intrusion into my thoughts?"

Silence met his inquiry and Phoenix was surprised by the regret he felt over being ignored. He wanted the femme in his life and was considering Gareth's modus by making Tristan his paramour. With too many fermented libations in his system, he closed his eyes and dreamed of Tristan Faire.

At the sun's rising, Phoenix awoke with his limbs entwined with Gareth's and Temple's. His head

118

pounded with a vengeance as he tried to recall when they had crawled into his bed. He was astonished to find himself covered in dried seminal fluids. Either they had painted him in their ejaculate, or his dreams of Tristan had become more graphic than usual, resulting in his orgasm, or his friends had convinced him to participate in their debauchery. *By the grace of the Divinity, I wish I could remember!*

He disentangled himself from the heavy bodies and escaped to the evacuation room. After emptying his system of the previous night's toxins, he stepped into the ion shower, longing for Tristan's luxurious tub to soothe his tired muscles.

Once he dressed and dried his long hair, he conformed to his usual ritual and sipped his effervescent libations while staring out of his floor-to-ceiling windows, viewing the metropolis below him. His gaze strayed to the outlying area, and he wondered about Terra Gaia and Wiccan Tall. He'd rarely had the opportunity to mingle with heteros and considered that he may have missed out on priceless opportunities to know his prefecture's citizenry.

Tristan and his mother shared the same irreverence for his station. They were both willing to stand up to him and express their opinions without regard for consequences. They were headstrong, a quality Phoenix was growing to appreciate. He had been surrounded by sycophants all his life, and he was now finding it refreshing to experience viewpoints different from his own. He liked how she called Tristan and the parents 'darling'. Until he'd met Tristan, pet names had been an unfamiliarity. He enjoyed hearing Tristan call him darling *and* love. Each time he used the endearments, Phoenix felt a thousand butterfly wings flittering in his stomach. When he heard Riley use 'love' and Terra 'darling' he realized where Tristan had acquired his effortless speech patterns.

As his pinnacle rotated, his gaze fell upon Hybridia. He thought about Tristan sitting in his aviary sipping his morning libations. He wondered if the sanctuary's butterflies had left their cocoons. *I would have enjoyed seeing their emergence.*

Come to me, love. I'm waiting.

Before he could determine if Tristan was sending him a message, Gareth and Temple interrupted with their noisy entrance into his morning idyll.

"Covfefe! I need some, *now.*" Gareth demanded, rubbing his brow. Behind him, Temple's pale lavender skin was mottled dijon-yellow, a sure sign he'd imbibed more than a Portside sailor on shore leave.

"I don't keep that disgusting brew on hand. All I have is Staquo fruit and effervescent libations."

"How can you not have covfefe? It's the latest trend, grown on the mayor's own estate."

"It's as vile as our mayor is corrupt."

"Phoenix!" Gareth and Temple shouted in unison, followed by dual pained groans. Phoenix chuckled at their miserable discomfort, glad he'd stopped imbibing when he had.

"It's true and you know it. He was caught purple-handed with his fingers in the till when he granted the land development contract to the Eastern Praetorian Consortium, rather than our Staquo industrialists. How long did he think he could get away with ignoring our laws?"

"When did you become so concerned about the politics of the prefecture?" Temple dared to ask.

"Oh, my Divinity! Do you not know me at all?" Phoenix couldn't hide his incredulity. He'd known Gareth and Temple since his first days at university. Now he had discovered they were virtual strangers.

"We thought we did? 'Fuck em and fellate em, Phoenix.' Isn't that how you introduced yourself the first day we met?"

"Gareth, that was how many spans ago? We were students, and I was studying the political sciences in preparation to *become* the mayor! How do you not recall this?"

"Most likely because of all the fucking and fellating we've shared over those same spans. Divinity, you were far more attractive as a bedmate and a friend before you visited Hybridia. What the infernal-regions happened to you?"

Temple looked to Gareth, who scowled. "I do recall him mentioning it once or twice, but his service term is spans from now. Why is he all worked up?" Gareth shrugged and sat, resting his head on folded arms as if it were too heavy to hold up any longer.

Frustrated with his friends' frivolous natures, Phoenix set out effervescent libations for them and lamented for the umpteenth time that the mayor's duplicity had been uncovered. The covfefe mogul was stepping down and going to prison camp, prompting Phoenix to forego his supporting internship and move straight into the mayoral position. In thirty-two auroras, the responsibility of Prefecture Staquo would rest on Phoenix's shoulders. He received no commiserate response from his randy friend, only a self-serving comment that the stories they could tell of fucking the new mayor might be good for a round or two plus a blow job at the libation house.

Tamping down his disgust, Phoenix gathered his holo-tablet and holo-phone. "I have to meet my parent. Be sure to secure the exits before you go," Phoenix said, calling for his transport to meet him at the street level. As he waited for the lift to take him to the lower floors, he wondered how he would govern effectively with his so-called friends pornifying their acquaintance for free libations. Perhaps he could assign them positions in the Outlying area. He might have considered it, if it weren't for Terra Gaia, Wiccan Tall and Riley and Loren Faire. They did not deserve the condemnation and derision accompanying Gareth and Temple.

His transport arrived and in no time, he stood in front of Doctor Galen Ashe's office. His parent had cleared a tiny measure of time for him in his busy schedule. But if today's visit was like the others, Phoenix would have barely enough time to say hello before Dr. Galen was summoned to an emergence in crisis.

"The incubation chambers are aging and must soon be replaced," the doctor said to whomever he was speaking to on the holo-phone. He saw Phoenix and gestured for him to take a seat before returning to his call. "I don't know where you'll get the mintage, but if they're not replaced, you'll lose next season's emergences... In truth, all the chambers in the prefecture are in the same deplorable condition... Yes, I'm aware the mayor cut your funding. Keep in mind that if yours and the other chambers aren't replaced, and soon, mascs will join femmes on the endangered species records."

Dr. Ashe turned to Phoenix and eyed him, taking in every detail of his appearance. Beneath his scrutiny, Phoenix squirmed. "You've been fornicating with those miscreants again." It wasn't a question he wanted to answer. Phoenix well knew his parent's dislike of his companions. "You look terrible. You need to disengage yourself from those two and keep good company."

"I'm beginning to think you may be right, sir."

"Hmpf. What's brought about this change?"

"I've met someone."

"I hope he's suitable and a strong partner. You'll need plenty of support in the coming days. I have no doubt you are ready to govern. It's what you've spent the last thirty spans preparing for."

"Do you really think I'm ready?"

"Don't go fishing for compliments, Phoenix. It's unbecoming. Now I must go, there is a crisis at the Portside emergence center."

Phoenix walked with Galen to the transport station and bid him good departure as he was whisked away to Portside. With his afternoon free and his thoughts consumed by Tristan, Phoenix found himself wandering toward Hybridia.

Chapter Eleven

If the Hybridian femmes thought it strange for the six-and-one-half-cubits tall masc to stride through their streets as if he owned them, they kept their comments to themselves. Phoenix noticed a few pointing and wondered if they remembered him from the scene Terra Gaia had made while Tristan Faire sat with his parents and himself at breakfast.

He tried smiling and greeting the citizenry, but they gave him a wide berth and went about their business. If Phoenix believed it was odd for the purlieu's populace to avoid him, he paid them no mind. His thoughts were filled with seeing Tristan again. His outward, confident strut was a façade, as he acknowledged to himself that he was quite lost in the maze of narrow streets. He thought if he started from the market, he might make his way to Tristan's house. When freesia and cinnamon carried on the breeze, he followed the scent, knowing Tristan's store was nearby.

His olfactory senses had better orientation than his feet, which had gotten him off-track, leaving him to follow the familiar scents to the promenade. Tired from walking, he sat on the easy bench where he'd first met Tristan to rest and retrieve his bearings. In his mind, he saw the streets where he had strolled alongside the good-looking femme. He recalled the Common was around the bend on the other side of the boardwalk. If he found the school and chapel, he'd know where he was and could locate Tristan's cottage.

Unlike his previous visit to the depository district, the cinfree no longer affected his libido. He relaxed, watching eager mascs going into the depositories, a few entering the doors with their obvious erections. Others looked about furtively, as if they didn't want to be seen requesting the services offered. He wondered how he had appeared to the casual onlooker sitting and observing the crowded street. Did they recognize him as the confused masc who worried for the future of his prefecture? Or did they only see the hedonist image he'd spent the last ten spans cultivating? He would need supportive personnel surrounding him and had thought Gareth and Temple might be part of his inner circle. But after the morning's revelations, he was rethinking the wisdom of their counsel.

While he was reconsidering his choices for advisors, he spotted a familiar figure striding across the promenade toward the common. He was surprised to see Gareth moving with agility and purpose. After their excessive night, he'd supposed his friend wouldn't have left his apartment until the sun was setting. Phoenix called out to him, but Gareth was too far away to hear him.

Phoenix rose and followed Gareth, whose towering frame dwarfed the smaller femmes, making it was easy to keep track of him. His quarry made a turn onto a colorful lane that looked familiar to Phoenix. He quickened his pace to catch up with his friend. He'd planned on asking him to join him for cooling libations, but got distracted by a flash of yellow in a shop window. Phoenix paused to admire the colorful songbird and realized he'd lost Gareth. Confident he now recognized the way to Tristan's, he stepped into the store. After a pleasant chat with the young femme working there, he walked out holding a gilded cage carrying a pair of the sunny-colored birds.

Assured he knew where he was headed, Phoenix imagined Tristan's expressive face lighting up when he presented him with his gift for the aviary. He was unprepared for the sounds that greeted him from within the cottage.

"That's it, yeah like that. Just like that. Suck it. Suck it hard." Gareth's growly voice sounded through an open window as Phoenix raised his hand to knock. He recognized that lascivious growl. It was the sound Gareth made before orgasming. Phoenix pushed open the door and saw Tristan—his Tristan—on his knees swallowing Gareth's massive cock.

"Phoenix? Come join us. Trissie here...he's the ultimate sucking machine," Gareth said as he continued fucking Tristan's mouth. Tristan wore only pantaloons while Gareth was fully clothed with his codpiece opened. He had wrapped his hands in the femme's braids, holding him captive and ensuring Tristan kept fellating him. Through a cloud of disbelief, Phoenix saw Tristan trying to escape, but Gareth kept him flush to his groin as he started coming.

"That's it, Trissie. Take it all and don't you spill a drop. Swallow it. Let the next mayor see how much you love drinking my cum."

Phoenix wanted to run away, but his feet stayed glued to the floor. The tableau before him was as mesmerizing as it was revolting, once he realized Tristan didn't have a choice. He could swallow or choke. Phoenix had had Gareth's cock down his throat numerous times. The masc didn't pull out until he'd emptied his ball sac and laughed when his distressed partners couldn't breathe. *Why hadn't I ever noticed or cared about my friend's sadistic nature?*

The birds' warbling reminded him he still held their cage. He set it down and turned to leave.

"What's wrong? Phoenix! Come on! Join us," Gareth called out, oblivious to his paramour's distress.

"No, that's all right. I apologize for intruding." Phoenix looked back once then ran, not understanding why seeing Gareth and Tristan together upset him so much. He and his friend had fucked bed partners together many times. Gareth, Temple and himself had become inseparable the last few spans, sharing beds, sexual favors and bed mates like they shared sustenance.

"Please don't go, love. Let me explain."

Phoenix placed his hands over his ears, hoping to shut out Tristan's voice. But the femme was relentless.

"Come back to me, love. Give me a chance to ease your mind."

"Get the fuck out of my head!" Phoenix shouted, unmindful of the strangers turning to gawk at him as if he were insanity-driven. Perhaps he was, because no one had ever disturbed his sense of self quite like Tristan Faire. Mindful of his consequence, he stopped running and ambled through the purlieu until he was hopelessly lost. He spotted a small tavern, the type of rough establishment he was known for avoiding. He glanced around and realized he'd left Hybridia and walked all the way to Portside. Needing to rest before returning to Segratia, Phoenix stepped inside the thick hewn doors.

The acrid stench of smoke sticks greeted him as he ambled across the tavern's threshold. He found a seat in a darkened corner and signaled the barkeep. A thin, unkempt hetero limped toward him and asked what he would like. His grizzled visage masked his curiosity as he peered at the high-emerged masc.

"Bring me a bottle of your finest fermented libation, please," Phoenix said, handing the proprietor mintage enough for two quality bottles.

"Fermented libation? Pfft. Gin all right by you?"

"Yes. Thank you."

"I dun think I can make change. This is more mintage than we score in three auroras. Dun you got anything smaller?"

"I'm afraid not. Don't worry about it. Keep the extra…for your family."

"Folks ain't usually so generous around these parts. What 'cha wants in kind? Sexual favors? Me missus might be willing to incubate your spawn, but then with this much mintage on ya, I reckon you could buy one of them fancy chambers."

"I can understand your reticence to take what you think of as charity, Mr. — "

"Dawson. Elton Dawson."

"Well, Mr. Dawson, like I was saying, I realize you may not appreciate philanthropy, so how about if you give me an hour of your time for the rest of the mintage?"

Elton looked at Phoenix as if he'd grown an extra head. He mumbled and limped back to the bar, returning with a full bottle of gin and two clean glasses.

"You're a strange one, aren't ya?" Elton took a seat across from Phoenix and doled out their drinks.

"You have no idea," Phoenix said, putting his elbows on the rough table and holding his head in his hands.

"Fair warning. I ain't given no blow jobs in thirty spans. Not since I met the missus. Knees ain't what they used to be and I'm certain you could buy the company of some fine attendant to see to your needs. So, what is it you want?" Elton slammed down his drink and poured another before lighting a smoke stick and drawing the vile stuff into his lungs. He offered one to Phoenix who shook his head and swallowed the gin, coughing at the fermentation's cold burn. Elton refilled their glasses and smiled. "Go ahead with your questions, boy."

Phoenix appreciated the man's candid manner and wondered about his surprising revelation that he used to fellate. He was interested in hearing about his troubles and hoped he could make him comfortable enough to share his story.

"I'm uncertain how to phrase this without appearing offensive. I've been considering the plight of the femmes, and their inability to ensure their line's continuation."

"Son, you gotta stop with the thousand-mintage words, if you want an old saloon keeper like me to keep up. I didn't get no fancy la-de-da education."

"I'm sorry. I'll try again."

"Ain't no need to apologize for being smart."

"Are you aware that the femme population in Hybridia is nearing extinction?"

"Explain egg...stink shun."

"It means their numbers are dying off faster than new femmes are emerged. There'll come a day when Staquo will no longer have any femmes."

"And you wanna know how I feel about that?" Phoenix nodded. "Why?"

"You're a citizen of the prefecture. Your opinion matters."

Elton snorted and laughed as if Phoenix were Jackson Lennox, the famous comedian he'd once seen performing in the common. "I'm sorry, son, but it's been at least twenty spans since I mattered to any masc."

"I am hoping to remedy that. Our prefecture is a tri-culture, meaning we have three distinct groups of people living here. The mascs, femmes and the heteros. It's recently been pointed out to me that the three are treated differently not only by each other, but also by their government."

"I s'pose, but that is the way things is, always has been. Back in the time, when I attended chapel, the Prelate would read from the great book, saying that was the will of the Divinity. Mascs were here to rule Gemin, femmes to serve and heteros... Well, with the techno-wonders we learned to just stay out of the way. But, our womenfolk, now they had something the others wanted, and they were revered for it. The men were tolerated."

"What did your women have? Riches?"

"No, boy. They had fertile wombs. In the ancient times, there were no incubation contraptions. No emergence chambers. Hetero womenfolk were charged with bearing the little ones and paid handsomely for it. But as the eons passed and techno-wonders became the new divinities, the ladies were no longer needed. Your kind, and to some measure, the femmes, incubated their babes in the modern machines, and the heteros faded away to the Outlying area."

"You know an enormous amount of Gemin history for an old barkeep."

"And you get awfully bold after two slugs of gin. Who you callin' old? I may be a fossil and a gimp, but I used to sail the seas and lived to bring home the tales. The missus and I run this place for Qandi Kane, an aging femme. He's a fancy pants kind of person. Likes to get all dudded up in finery and sit at this very table, telling stories of his visits to the common for the display parades."

"The display parade?" Phoenix swallowed his gin, savoring the burn and trying in vain to hide behind the half-empty bottle.

"Yepper. Enjoys ogling the femmes working the mascs into a frenzy of need, the likes which I haven't experienced in a bushel of spans. Sometimes I go with him to pass out flyers advertising the tavern's after-parade specials. Made the trip 'bout a hunert auroras ago, during the twin solstice."

"You did?" Phoenix squeaked, refilling Elton's glass and topping off his own.

"Seems I recollect there was a large masc, about your height, with long flowing white hair, much like yours. The femmes with him put on quite a spectacle, to the point the poor fellow was shouting 'Ibis' and had to be carried off the stage."

"Why are you telling me this?"

"Son, I may be hetero and I may be old, but my eyes are keen and my mind sharp. I keep up with current events, especially those that can affect me and mine. I recognized you as soon as you came through the door, looking like you were running from the infernal-region's demons. I also know you will be the next mayor."

"Oh...my...Divinity," Phoenix lamented, closing his eyes from the sharp gaze leveled at him. How could he explain what had happened and why he was here in Portside? Elton was a barkeep, and Phoenix's experience with mixologists had shown him they liked to gossip. "All I wanted to do was get your opinion on the social structure of the prefecture. Now I will lose my credibility before I take the mayoral oath. I'm doomed."

"No need for the dramatics, boy. Your secret's safe with me. Here, let me top off your glass, and you go right ahead and unburden yourself to old Elton."

With what he'd consumed the previous night, and his intake of gin before sunset, Phoenix could not contain himself. He talked and talked and when Bernie—short for Bernice—Dawson joined them, he told her all about Tristan, and his parents, and his mother, and his cock down Gareth's throat, and the birds he had left singing on the floor of Tristan's cottage. The plump, blowsy woman listened as if she'd never heard such a woeful tale. When Phoenix ran out of words and could no longer hold up his head, she took him up the rickety stairs and put him to bed on the straw mattress.

"Me boy slept here, before he sailed the Paradrae Sea to make his fortune. You should be comfortable enough."

"Thank you. Your solishus...solicitshus...kindness is 'preciated," Phoenix said. "I fear I've overindulged, my good lady. My profound apologies."

Bernie's giggle was the last thing he heard before closing his eyes.

Phoenix awoke to the sounds of revelry from the tavern below. He groaned, rubbing the sleep from his eyes. He didn't recognize his surroundings. As he looked around the tiny sparse room, he noticed the bed was too small for his large frame as he grinned at his feet hanging off the end. His head throbbed and he needed water to ease his thirst. *Gin. What was I thinking?* The demon's brew had never been kind to him.

Phoenix rose from the bed, ran his fingers through his tangled hair and went searching for the evacuation room. Easily locating the small chamber, he took care of his business, rinsed his mouth and tried to bring some semblance of order to his hair. Deciding he'd done his best, he crept downstairs, hoping he could leave before anyone saw him.

"There you are, boy. I almost felt guilty for pouring that last jigger of gin, but figured you had paid for it tenfold, so why not enjoy? Sit. I'll have the missus bring you a bite," Elton said in a voice much too cheerful to believe he had imbibed half a bottle of the demon drink with him earlier.

"Thank you, Mr. Dawson, but I really must go."

"Good evenin', lovey. Feeling better, are you?" Bernie asked while she straightened the collar on his shirt. "Let ole Bernie bring you a little sustenance before you leave us. Come. There's someone I want you to meet."

Embarrassed to refuse the woman's kindness, even though his stomach clenched at the mention of sustenance, Phoenix let her lead him to the table he and Elton had occupied earlier. Seated on the bench was an aged femme, flamboyantly dressed in silken shirt and pantaloons, with feathered boas draping his arms. On each finger, he wore bright sparkling rings of precious Outlying gemstones. His shoes were forest-green slippers, and he smelled like cinfree, pine and cannabis smoke. His bright smile showed even, yellowing teeth and cheerful eyes with genuine warmth in their kohl-lined depths. He wore his hair in the braids favored by the femmes.

"Qandi Kane, this here is Phoenix Ashe, the handsome young masc I was telling you about," Bernie said as she tugged Phoenix forward on his reluctant feet.

"How do you do, sir."

"I do just fine, sonny. Sit down and let an old femme get a good look at you. Bernie and Elton tell me you have questions and I might help you. Been a long time since a fine, strong masc needed my help. Bernie, send over a bottle and two glasses. You know what I like."

"Sure thing. But take it easy on the youngster, he needs sustenance first." Bernie sidled off to the bar, pouring drinks for several waiting customers before returning with their order. Phoenix groaned inwardly at the full bottle of gin and the bowl of oryx stew he was expected to eat. She also set down a round loaf of blue-grain bread. Phoenix grimaced at the thought of food.

"Don't worry, lovey. The bread will soak up the gin and keep you from spilling your guts all over your fancy boots."

"Go ahead, eat up," Qandi said, leaning back and peering at him to ensure he followed Bernie's directive.

He tore off a piece of the bread, then dipped it into the stew. Savoring the bite, Phoenix was surprised at the remarkable flavor. In moments, he'd sopped up the last of the juices and licked his fingers clean. He blushed when he glanced up and saw his companion staring at him with his mouth agape.

"Don't believe I've ever seen a high-emerged masc do *that* before," Qandi said before bursting into gleeful laughter. "It's good to know our next mayor is as base as his constituency."

"Does *everyone* know who I am?" Phoenix asked in mortification.

"Don't get all worked up, lovey. Me and the Dawsons are the only ones who know your little secret. But why you are slumming here in Portside has me flummoxed."

Phoenix began to think they'd put something in his food, or perhaps it was the Portside gin, because he heard himself talking to Qandi as if he'd known him all his spans and they were the best of friends. It was easy to forget that like all the femmes he knew, this one was also a telepath. He asked all the right questions and was unfazed by whatever Phoenix said.

"What you're saying to me is that you and Tristan Faire experienced transcendence the first night you stayed with him. And you hadn't had intimate relations with him prior to then?"

"Other than the inaugural deposit...no. The display parade preparation was all carried out by Dorian Seaborn."

"Interesting," Qandi said, as he filled their glasses and handed Phoenix a bit of bread. Phoenix discovered that the sustenance kept his head from becoming heavy and instead of a need to dispel his stomach's contents, a warm soothing feeling infused his being and loosened his tongue.

"That's all you have to say? Interesting?"

"Spans ago, when I was young and beautiful, I worked at the depositories. I held Tristan's same title — premier attendant — and I was most revered. The adoration of the clientele for our carnal skills and the notoriety among our peers was intoxicating. A femme can either thrive on it, or he becomes restless for something more meaningful — a committed relationship. When this happens and if he finds his chosen partner — transcendence.

"The femmes managing the depositories are very powerful telepaths. They know when their attendants have become restless before the attendant recognizes his own discontent. They use their knowledge to sell exorbitant bonding packages to their clients."

"But what about the client purchasing the services, is he ready for a committed partnership?"

"It doesn't matter. They use aromatics and telepathy to manipulate the client. The attendant is unaware of their manipulations, and both walk away bonded and happy."

Hot anger churned in Phoenix to hear he had been a victim of such vile emotional machinations.

"Calm down. There is a natural, I suppose you could call it a failsafe that the Divinity gave us to ensure a masc and femme's compatibility and happiness. And that is transcendence. You see, the phenomenon does not occur unless both parties are willing and in love. If it doesn't happen, the client goes home, believing he had the most profound intimate experience of his life."

"Fuck you. I'm not in love with Tristan and he doesn't love me!"

"What would you say if I told you that transcendence normally requires at least five full days and nights of conversation and fucking before it's possible?"

Open-mouthed and wide-eyed, Phoenix stared at Qandi in silence until his eyes burned. He reached for his glass with trembling fingers.

"You and Tristan transcended after *one* day — away from the artifices of the depository. Think about *that*."

Chapter Twelve

Tristan sat alone on his divan in the gray dark, with nothing but the holo-screen illuminating the room, and the sounds of waves kissing the shoreline mocking him. He'd been a fool to have let Gareth Knightly, the masc he knew as Finn Lord, into his home. Finn had been a frequent Seminal Depository visitor who had become one of his regular clients.

Tristan had liked Finn well enough and when had grown restless, he'd asked Finn if he wanted to try something different, rather than only fellatio. At first, Finn had accepted the intimacies Tristan initiated. He'd enjoyed penetration with the polymer staffs, but had soon demanded to progress to fucking Tristan, often entering his ass without sufficient preparation. Despite numerous protests to his managers that Finn had hurt him, they'd ignored his protests and continued assigning him to the high-emerged masc. Following their encounters, Finn had always left extra mintage for Tristan, which he kept as his due for tolerating the less pleasant aspects of their appointments.

Thirty auroras before the twin solstice, Finn had leased a pleasure room at the depository where he and Tristan spent a week fucking and talking between orgasms. Tristan recalled Finn had been lighthearted and more considerate of Tristan's needs. He'd teased him mercilessly, using many of the same techniques Tristan had perfected for his clients. Each orgasm they'd shared had been exquisite, leaving him and Finn ensconced in a cloud of carnal bliss. Tristan had begun to consider that he may have found his mate and hoped Finn felt the same.

The final day of his stay, Tristan learned Seminal had contracted him to the masc for extra-curricular services. He'd considered refusing, but the previous night during intimacy, they had come a hairsbreadth away from transcendence. Tristan had grabbed the opportunity to spend even more time with Finn, hoping that he would eventually cross over into its perfect subliminal plane.

The arrangement had worked out to be satisfactory, with Tristan venturing into Segratia once to stay the evening at Finn's luxurious apartment. The other two encounters, Finn had come to his cottage. They'd never reached the intimate pinnacle they had before, but since he had quit Seminal, Tristan was happy with the added mintage.

What Phoenix had walked in on today was Tristan fulfilling the last encounter of his contract. He'd received a missive from Seminal that if he serviced Finn Lord this last time, they would consider his contracted obligation to them complete. Though in his mind he was committed to Phoenix, Tristan couldn't turn down the opportunity to be done with Seminal and Finn

Lord. He had agreed, never dreaming Phoenix would show up on his threshold.

Bad enough Phoenix had found him on his knees with a mouth full of cock, but to learn Finn Lord was Gareth Knightly made him sick of stomach. He and Phoenix had achieved transcendence the last time they had been together. In the femme's world, the experience was tantamount to a committed relationship. In Tristan's mind, Phoenix had discovered him committing adultery — with his best friend — and he was ashamed.

After Finn...Gareth left, appearing too smug for his liking, Tristan had spent the rest of the day reaching out to Phoenix through their psychic link. It amazed him how Phoenix could block his voice. He'd never known someone who could so effortlessly shut him out. Though Phoenix had refused to answer, he recognized his wandering steps had taken him into Portside where he'd spent the afternoon with Tristan's long-time friends Elton and Bernie Dawson. He knew Bernie would mother him to pieces, so he withdrew from his thoughts to concentrate on what he should do next to win Phoenix's affections.

There would be no easy answers coming to him tonight, so with a heavy sigh, he went to the aviary to check on the songbirds Phoenix had left. He wondered what it meant that the gorgeous masc had come to him with birds in hand.

Fuck you, Finn Lord. You've ruined everything!

Tristan rubbed his eyes and shook his head. He was mature enough to recognize that what had happened wasn't Finn's doing. After all, they'd had an enforceable contract, and he didn't believe Finn had intended any malice by showing up at his door before

Phoenix's arrival. Still, Finn, or rather Gareth, was an easy target for Tristan's frustrations.

The thick air hit him like it always did each time he entered the aviary. He had left the golden birds in their cage, letting them adapt to the aviary's environment. He made certain they had food and water before covering the coop with a cloth. On the morrow he would release them to join their feathered cousins in the trees.

"Good eventide, darling."

"Mother, are you wanting to apologize?"

"I sensed your melancholy and wanted to check that all is well. I'm sorry to intrude."

Tristan smiled, marveling at how adept she was at avoiding a direct question. She would have made a good politician had she not been born hetero.

"Not true. I would have hung the fool who sanctioned the depositories by the balls until they fell off."

"Why are you targeting the depositories?"

"My darling, they are the source of your unhappiness, and what makes you sad earns my anger."

"Are you going to apologize?"

"Of course. I'm sorry you're sad and hurting. Can I do anything to help?"

"Please explain how you got through to my thoughts. I did ban you."

"I'm your mother. You can't ban me. You understand this, Tristan. Although that was quite a show you put on for your masc's benefit."

"It wasn't for him. You made me so angry, calling me a whore, that I forgot you're like resin on my shoe. I can't get rid of you."

"No, you can't, and you would do well to remember that. I am and will always be your greatest ally."

"You are, and I love you dearly. I have missed you."

"As I've missed you, my darling. Now tell me, what's wrong."

"It's Phoenix."

"I thought as much. What has he done?"

"He hasn't done a thing. It's me. I messed up and I don't know how to fix the breach between us." Tristan waited for Terra to say something, but he was met with silence. He sensed her presence in his thoughts, waiting for him to elaborate. *"We experienced transcendence."*

"Oh. Well that certainly puts a different spin on the budding romance, doesn't it? I didn't realize your liaison had progressed to that point."

"Me either. But since our meeting at the depository, he's been searching for me. He came to Hybridia fourteen times before we connected. We spent the afternoon walking and talking, and he wanted to experience stage three of Seminal's menu of services." Tristan paused waiting for Terra to comment, but she just told him to continue. *"I had sensed his need for spiritual intimacy when he visited the depository, and I couldn't say no to him when he asked me to show him. I thought we'd have a pleasant interlude, because he would only commit to three nights with me. But that first night, oh my Divinity."*

"I don't want the details. I expect you achieved transcendence?"

"Yes! After just one night. But before I could explain what it meant for me and him, you and the parents showed up. After you and Wiccan left us that day in the establishment, Phoenix returned to Segratia."

"Then today, he found you servicing his friend."

"How did you know?"

"Your shout of anguish alerted me that something painful happened. I've been listening to you since then."

"What am I going to do, Mother?"

"On the morrow, go to him and explain. If he is unwilling to forgive or understand, bring him here to the farm."

"If he's resistant, how will I persuade him to come with me?"

"Tell him I can help him with the changes he wants to make in the prefecture."

"What?"

"Think, Tristan. Phoenix is about to become mayor. He is young and without experience governing. On top of that, he feels he's been betrayed by his friend and he's confused about his feelings for you. At our last meeting, we gave him something to think about that has made him question all he was taught to believe. He needs counsel and whether he believes it or not, we're the ones who can provide it."

"I'm sure you're right, but it will not be an easy task persuading him to come."

"Oh, my darling. I have every confidence you can get him to come." With her ringing laughter pealing in his head, Tristan broke their connection, pondering how he could convince Phoenix to forgive him.

In the morning, with a small portmanteau in hand, he stepped out into the promising sunrise and called for a transport. One way or another, Phoenix Ashe was going to listen to him.

Chapter Thirteen

"Go away. Quit bothering me," Phoenix grumbled, turning over in his bed and covering his throbbing head with his pillow.

"Good daybreak, love. Time to awaken."

"Leave me be," Phoenix protested. He'd gotten in late, and with a system full of gin, dawn was too fucking early for the sun to rise. He vowed that for his first mayoral act, he would initiate midnight savings time. Longer sleeping hours was what the people needed.

A low, growly snicker told him how ridiculous he was being. He cursed Qandi Kane for his abused condition. Another sultry laugh went straight to his groin. He rubbed his cock as it hardened, reminding him how much he'd missed Tristan's talented mouth.

"I would love to take care of that for you."

"I don't need you. Go back to Gareth and suck him."

Tristan's wry chuckle irritated him, and though he realized he was being childish and Tristan couldn't see him, he flipped him his middle digit. The coarse and unsuitable behavior for an upcoming mayor gave Phoenix a small measure of satisfaction at expressing his pique. He resumed idly stroking his cock until the doorbell's ringing interrupted him. Cursing because now he *had* to get out of bed, he threw a robe over his nudity and padded into the entryway to answer the insistent peal.

"Tristan! What the fuck are you doing here?"

"Good daybreak, Phoenix Ashe."

"How did you sneak past the lower floor security? And why aren't you in Hybridia?"

"Kiss me first, then I'll explain."

"No. Absolutely not!" Mindful of his excited state beneath the robe, Phoenix knew Tristan would soon notice. After all, his skin had just turned a darker lavender before he'd answered the door. Disgruntled with Tristan's arrival, Phoenix blocked his entry.

Phoenix crossed his arms, daring Tristan to get past him. He tried ignoring his erection and was certain Tristan could smell his arousal. He didn't expect his obstinate behavior to deter Tristan. He was well aware of Phoenix's condition, since he'd just been poking around in his mind. Catching him off guard, Tristan slipped a hand into Phoenix's robe, loosening the tie and grasping his leaking cock.

"Now, you may let me in, or I'll go to my knees here in your prestigious doorway and suck your shaft until your ecstatic shouts are echoing through the halls." Phoenix received the vision Tristan sent him — a mental flash of Phoenix wildly fucking Tristan's mouth and screaming his name. Phoenix's skin darkened, his breathing quickened, and his cock throbbed hot and hard in Tristan's palm.

The door to the next apartment opened. His neighbor stepped into the hallway and gave them a disapproving glance. Femme's were an anomaly in their high-rise building and judging from his deep frown, the old masc didn't appreciate Tristan's presence.

Phoenix shrugged off his robe and wrapped Tristan in his arms, kissing him long and hard. He heard the shocked and outraged sounding gasp from the nosy neighbor as he headed for the lower floor lift. Phoenix wondered if his enthusiasm in greeting Tristan wasn't a result of the censure directed at them, rather than his delight at Tristan's arrival. Before he could analyze his motives, Tristan patted his cheek and drew his attention.

"I like your exuberance, love," Tristan said disentangling himself from Phoenix's embrace. "I see you've been enjoying Elton's evil toxins."

"Have you been spying on me?"

"No. You were quite efficient in shutting me out of your thoughts. However, the Dawsons' gin is odiferous in its own unique way."

"You're saying I smell."

"I think it's known as aurora breath." Tristan chuckled, giving Phoenix a kiss on his stubbled cheek. "Go and freshen up, and I'll fix you a libation that will cure your nagging headache."

The promise of making the ache in his temples disappear motivated Phoenix to shower, shave and clean his teeth — twice. He returned, wrapped in his robe, to find Tristan sitting at his polymer table, staring out at the entrancing view from the pinnacle. His heart stuttered as he pictured Tristan preparing libations every daybreak. In his mind, they would chat after a morning of passionate intimacies before he left to pursue his busy schedule. It was a domestic picture he liked but acknowledged as being unrealistic. They were masc and femme. Though they could share carnal delights, mascs were destined for mascs and femmes for femmes. It was the way of their world. *The Divinity's directive is clear, isn't it?*

Phoenix wondered what filled Tristan's thoughts before he turned and stared at him with something unfamiliar in his eyes. A soft smile tilted his lips, tempting Phoenix to kiss him again. Beneath his sharp scrutiny, Phoenix shuffled from foot to foot, but he couldn't tear his gaze away as he tried to decipher Tristan's expression.

"You look gorgeous. Come have a seat," Tristan said, taking Phoenix's hand and leading him to a chair. He handed him a tall, cold glass filled with a lime-green liquid. He sipped it and the tart effervescent burst on his tongue. "Drink up, love. You'll feel much better once you're finished."

"What are you doing here?" Phoenix sipped his libation, acknowledging its restorative powers. Tristan didn't answer him, instead he pulled a brush from a portmanteau sitting on the floor. He began brushing Phoenix's long hair dry. He ran the bristles through the damp locks as he spoke through their psychic bond.

"I've missed you. I feared you wouldn't come back. But then you did, and you brought me the wonderful songbirds. I love them. I wished you had been there to see how happy they were to fly up into the trees. No longer caged, they sing in harmony with the other birds."

"I would have enjoyed seeing them, too. But all I could envision was you on your knees with Gareth's cock in your mouth," Phoenix scoffed. Despite the sensuality of the brush's glide through his locks, he couldn't let go of his resentment.

"Yes, I understand. But why are you so angry? You knew I was an attendant and everything it entailed. Is it because you are acquainted with Gareth?" Tristan dropped their connection and spoke aloud, realizing Phoenix's anger hampered his ability to converse telepathically.

"Gareth had said he was visiting a femme regularly in Hybridia. He raved about his oral skills, but I never guessed *you* were the one he called upon. It threw me, that's all."

"So, it's his duplicitous nature that has you riled?"

"Not really. I know what Gareth is and what he isn't. I discovered more about him and Temple yesterday than I'm comfortable knowing."

"Do you want to tell me about it?" Tristan asked, turning Phoenix in his chair to face him. He held his gaze and waited for Phoenix to answer, fingering the silken strands of his hair. "Mmm, you smell like rain-kissed starglow petals." Tristan nuzzled Phoenix's neck, savoring the scent of the tiny white flowers which blanketed the Outlying meadows. They were revered for their heady fragrance, which often drifted into the city on the mountain breezes.

"You shouldn't do that. It's inappropriate for us to continue any sort of liaison. You're femme and I'm masc," Phoenix protested, sounding just as haughty as he had the afternoon Tristan had come upon him on the promenade.

"Hmm. What if I told you…I'm okay with you being masc?" Tristan teased. Phoenix glared at him, lifting one eyebrow and gritting his teeth. Tristan ignored his chagrin and eyed him up and down, taking in his darkening complexion and growing erection "I mean, everyone can't be perfect. Besides, you are kind of cute, even with all that purple skin."

Phoenix glanced at his hands and saw that, despite his irritation with Tristan, his skin had darkened, and his cock *was* demanding attention between his robe's folds. What was it about this annoying femme that excited him like no other? He should've demanded he leave and return to Hybridia. There was no future for them, nor was he certain he deserved one.

"Liar. You want the same future I do. You and me together, shocking the good citizens of Staquo with our unorthodox romance. You thirst for it, the same as me. It's why you came searching for me in Hybridia and it's why you came to my cottage bearing gifts."

"You shouldn't listen in on my thoughts. It's unnerving and invasive." Phoenix chastised, knowing it wouldn't do any good. "Even if what you say is true, there's no point. You may become my paramour, but you can never be my partner. The prelate would not sanctify our union. You are femme and I am masc."

"What does that matter, love?"

"Not only is our affair against Divinity doctrine, it's also frowned on by Gemin laws. Though not formally outlawed, a mixed intimacy is strongly discouraged."

"I still don't see the problem. So, we're mixed, together we'd be formidable."

"In less than thirty auroras I will be Segratia's mayor. I cannot do anything to sully my image if I'm to govern effectively."

"I believe you underestimate your constituency, love. There are more blended liaisons than you are aware.

But let's not argue. There are other numerous more pleasant ways to communicate."

Tristan sank to his knees and opened Phoenix's robe, taking a moment to admire the defined muscles, the tempting divot amid the ripples and the platinum trail of hair leading to a nest of white curls. He salivated as he gazed at the thick cock, beckoning him with its pearlescent bead of pre-seminal fluid. He leaned forward and took Phoenix into his mouth. Humming and tonguing his slit, Tristan sent him his thoughts.

"Your flavor is extraordinary, like the sweetest Staquo fruit."

Phoenix's heady moans encouraged Tristan to continue.

"I love how your cock stretches my lips like no other. You were made for my oral pleasure. Fuck my mouth. Let me feel and taste your pleasure."

Phoenix groaned and widened his legs, allowing Tristan better access to his opening and ball sac.

"What would it hurt for another interlude before you go?"

"I'm not going anywhere, love. At least, not until I've quenched my thirst for you."

Tristan reveled in Phoenix's easy acquiescence, lapping his balls and teasing his opening. When he swallowed his cock again, Phoenix grabbed onto his hair and lifted his hips from the chair thrusting into his mouth.

"Oh, Divinity. The fiery warmth of your mouth is too much. I feel like I'm falling and only you are keeping me grounded. Please."

Tristan sucked harder reveling in his masc's cries. *"I'll catch you. Let go and feed me your essence."*

Tristan's scalp stung as Phoenix tightened his grip on his hair and plunged harder into his mouth. His lips were stretched to their limit as he took the punishing assault and swallowed every thirst-quenching drop, all the while sending Phoenix endearments and loving promises. When Phoenix had finished, Tristan held his hand and led him into the bedroom. Tristan threw aside the rumpled sheets then pushed Phoenix onto the bed. He knelt and settled Phoenix's calves over his shoulders. He lapped at his opening, breaching it with his tongue and nibbling the sensitive skin, taking pleasure in the ever-darkening complexion.

"Come on, love. Open for me. Show me how much you desire me."

Tristan inserted one spit-wetted finger, then two, as Phoenix grasped the sheets and pushed back against his insistent intrusion. When he added a third finger, Phoenix cried out.

"Burns. Oh Divinity! So good…so fucking good."

Tristan stood and, without warning, plunged into Phoenix, fucking his depths and hitting his pleasure gland with each precise stroke.

"Look at me, Phoenix. Open your eyes and watch me…watch us." Beneath Tristan the glistening, diamond-dusted skin of his lover shimmered in the morning light. Phoenix lifted his passion-heavy lids and locked his gaze with Tristan. His sable-hued eyes darkened to black, signaling the approach of another orgasm. Tristan fucked him, driving himself mad with each sure glide of his cock. He stared in wonder at the beautiful masc whose obsidian gaze bored into his soul. Tristan read Phoenix's desires as the masc chased another Gemin-shattering climax. Tristan gritted his

C.L. Etta

teeth, concentrating on holding back his own orgasm until he had assured himself of Phoenix's pleasure.

As Phoenix neared the zenith, he heard Tristan babbling in his head. *"Come, love. Give yourself to me. Let me love you. I'll stand by your side forever. You're my chosen partner, the one I love. The one I'll always love."* He wanted to submit, give Tristan what he asked for, but he'd been conditioned for thirty spans. Masc for masc. Femme for femme. Tristan's impassioned voice filled his thoughts, driving out Phoenix's insecurities, until all he noticed was the trembling of his body and the insatiable need to commit to his pretty femme.

Phoenix's initial inclination to reject Tristan's sweet promises slipped away as he fell into a vortex of longing stronger than his discriminatory instincts. He coveted what Tristan was offering him, a relationship that was for him alone, unimaginable pleasure at his hands and an eternity of bliss. He craved Tristan's love.

"For Divinity's sake, don't stop fucking me!" Too aroused to speak, Phoenix surrendered his thoughts to Tristan.

"Never, love, for you're mine. My home."

"Tristan, please."

"What is it you need?"

"For you to love me."

"Always, until we're done making a lifetime of treasured memories."

With Tristan's words warming his heart and his sexual prowess gratifying his body, Phoenix came with a shout, his powerful release taking Tristan with him into a massive climax.

Tristan pulled Phoenix to him, claiming his lips in a heated kiss. Tongues and teeth clashed as they struggled to get even closer. As Phoenix's warm ejaculate erupted between them, he felt Tristan emptying his seminal fluids.

Tristan collapsed onto Phoenix, encompassing him into his embrace. Phoenix nestled into the arms around him, satiated and incapable of coherent thought. Lying face-to-face in joint solitude, he waited for his erratic heartbeat to slow. Now that his body's needs had been met and he'd caught his breath, Phoenix's thoughts raced with doubts.

Tristan brushed the strands of sweat dampened hair from Phoenix's face. "Tell me what you're thinking."

"You could read my mind for yourself," Phoenix scoffed.

"I could, but I'd rather you let me know what's troubling you."

Phoenix drew his eyebrows together, and he bit his lip, struggling with his reply. He met Tristan's steady gaze and asked. "What did you mean by saying, I am your home?"

"Do you know the tale of Arlo the wandering minstrel?"

"I heard it once when I was an adolescent. Why? What does an ancient fable of an old man have to do with us and what you said?"

"Do you remember how it ends?"

"When the man tired of his travels, he returned home to live out his days among his people."

"But do you recall what the final line of the anecdote was?"

"No."

"And home Arlo came from a weary road, with accolades of fame to a lonely hearth, until he noticed Beckham shadowed in the corner, a welcome smile to greet him and open arms to hold him. Long had it been since he'd known such warmth, a man with strength enough to still his wandering feet. With lips of nectar soft and sweet, he kissed his man and succumbed to the promise of a welcome body and happy life. With only Beckham was there transcendence."

The moments ticked by as Phoenix digested the tale's end. He had never heard the final line, and he told Tristan the version he'd heard ended with 'happy life'. "Why are you telling me this tale? What has it to do with us?"

"You are my Beckham. With no other but you, Phoenix Ashe, is there transcendence."

"I'm not certain how I feel about that. I mean transcendence was incredible, but are you saying you can't achieve that level of…I don't know…stimulation with anyone else? Didn't you and Gareth — ?"

"Hush, I don't want to speak of him, not when you are in my arms and your spend dries on my skin. But, to answer your question — no, you are the only one with whom I've transcended. There will be no others."

Reading sincerity in his brilliant blue eyes, Phoenix acknowledged his powerful attraction to the pretty femme. He leaned in and kissed Tristan, cupping his cheek and wondering how they would ever make a life together.

Chapter Fourteen

Tristan read the doubt in Phoenix's thoughts even as he returned his kiss. That was all right. He also tasted acceptance and, at least for now, there was trust. Love would come later. Phoenix had a lifetime of preconceived notions to shed before he'd fully accept they belonged together. Tristan realized his family would help Phoenix understand how they could coexist in Phoenix's world.

After a shower comprised of mutual blow jobs and enticing kisses, Phoenix and Tristan sat in the main living quarters while the robo-servant set out an afternoon repast of sandwiches and fruit. The libations were citrus-filled and their restorative qualities invigorating.

"Are you able to take a week from your schedule and accompany me to visit my parents?" Tristan asked as he set down his glass and studied Phoenix's surprised expression.

"To the Outlying areas?" Phoenix replied, making it sound as if Tristan had requested his presence at a beheading.

"Yes. It's where they live."

"I can't get away but maybe three auroras. Why?"

"I'd like for you to spend time with them and the others. You'll see we femmes aren't such a bad lot and there's more to us than our fellating skills. Besides, Wiccan and Terra are eager to know you. And my mother owes you her apology."

"I've never doubted that you possessed more abilities than those of a depository attendant. I've not expressed a negative thought or word about the femme community. I'm hurt you believe so."

"I'm very sorry, love. The last thing I would want to do is dishearten you when I wish to own your heart. But if three auroras are all you can give me, I'll accept it, provided we leave right away."

"I have communications to make before I'm free to go. Perhaps you should gather your things while I take care of my obligations."

"I have all I need with me." At Phoenix's puzzled expression, Tristan explained, "I had high hopes you would join me, so I came prepared. The birds have plenty of food and the aviary has a fresh water spring. I'll wait for you here and let Mother know we're coming."

Tristan read Phoenix's confusion over his easy acquiescence to his maneuverings. He felt bad for his apprehensions, but didn't have a single regret over their— What had Phoenix called it? *Oh, yes. An interlude.* With a small smile, he watched Phoenix disappear into his office to complete his business. Unmindful of his blatant eavesdropping, he listened in to Phoenix informing the Segratian hierarchy of his sojourn to the Outlying area.

He watched Phoenix packing and listened to him pondering the Segratians' disgruntled attitudes over his intended visit.

As Phoenix gathered his belongings, Tristan spied him noticing a golden choker with a jeweled pendant next to his portmanteau. Before Phoenix could question its presence, Tristan asked him to wear it. Phoenix picked it up and turned it over in his hand. He frowned.

"This aquamarine jewel looks familiar," Phoenix mumbled. "Is it the same pendant I wore for the display parade?"

Tristan nodded, hoping the sparkling lights of the gem would attract Phoenix. Tristan smiled with satisfaction as he fastened it around Phoenix's neck, settling the stone in his throat's hollow. He closed and locked his portmanteau and faced Tristan.

"I'm ready. Shall I call for a transport?"

Tristan couldn't tear his gaze away from his pendant and grinned. The sight of his lover wearing his jewels excited him almost as much as the masc himself.

"Already taken care of, love. It's picking us up here on the sky level."

"Wonderful. It's been a while since I've used skyport conveyances. I generally take the ground transport even though it takes longer."

"There is a certain intrigue with street level travel, but for the lengthy trip to Canopia, the village where my parents and Mother reside, I prefer the air. Are you ready?"

Tristan grabbed his portmanteau and Phoenix entered the door's security code. Tristan rarely traveled by skyport, since the buildings in Hybridia lacked the towering presence of the ones in Segratia. He lifted his face into the wind and gazed out over the impressive city.

"Why do you prefer the ground transports?"

Phoenix blushed. "Heights make me dizzy, an embarrassing characteristic I've kept to myself for thirty spans."

"How have you managed to do that?"

"By telling my friends I prefer to mingle with the masses. They took me at my word when I explained walking among the Segratian mascs would keep me humble and make me a better mayor."

Tristan held on to Phoenix's arm, sensing his apprehension. They were one-hundred-forty stories above the ground, standing on a clear polymer platform. Below them, private transports filled the mid-lane, while the street level traffic was at a standstill. The upper lanes were reserved for commercial travel.

"Why do you occupy the pinnacle tower, if you're uncomfortable with heights?"

"Who said I'm afraid?"

"Telepath here. Remember? And I didn't say you were *afraid*. I said 'uncomfortable'."

"It's expected."

"Who expects you to live in the clouds if you don't like heights?"

"My parent, the Segratian hierarchy, my friends, the Segratian populace. Besides, none of them realize I dislike the higher altitudes. I have a reputation of strength to maintain."

"Sometimes admitting your weaknesses is a greater show of strength than hiding them."

"A ridiculous adage to which no masc would ever adhere."

Tristan decided not to argue, knowing there would be plenty of time to convince his lover otherwise. "Are you okay with the air transportation I've arranged? If you like, we can change to ground level. I wouldn't want you miserable."

"I'm with you. How can I be anything but content?"

Phoenix's tender remark warmed Tristan's heart as he noted that the comment was the nicest thing he had said to him. Before he replied, their transport arrived. He put his and Phoenix's bags into the luggage compartment before taking Phoenix's hand and assisting him into the luxurious seats. He slipped a tiny disc into the vehicle's computer center. While he had waited for Phoenix to complete his business, Tristan had programmed the preferred route to Canopia, along with selected melodies. He planned to narrate their trip himself and if he was lucky, by the time they reached Tristan's home, Phoenix would have a deeper understanding of the Outlyers.

Once they were settled, the transport glided away from the platform and into the sparse afternoon traffic of the upper level. Phoenix avoided looking down except to point out the mayoral mansion he would move into within weeks. He also showed Tristan City Hall, where he'd spend his days governing.

"Are you ready to delve into the mayoral seat? What about the current supporting mayor? Shouldn't he be stepping into the head position?"

"Normally, yes. But the improprieties implicated Greyson Stiff, too. The council asked him to step down or face prosecution."

"Then who is next in the line of succession?"

"There has never been a scandal of this proportion and the prefecture's charter calls only for a mayor and supporting mayor. The Council decided, since I had not yet moved into the governing circle, my unconventional naïveté may be a better choice than taking a chance and appointing someone from within who may also be jaded."

"I understand. The council's decision reflects highly upon you. To trust someone who has no government experience with so much responsibility is unusual."

"Truth is, most of them have known my parent for many spans. Which means they are familiar with me, and I interned in the council while I completed my studies. I'm not a complete unknown."

"You'll make a wonderful mayor, love. Of that, I am certain."

Tristan handed Phoenix a cold libation. As Phoenix sipped the refreshment, he noted they were leaving the city limits and traveling through the Outlying area. Phoenix kept his attention on his drink and avoided looking out of the transport's windows.

When the Paradrae Sea came into view in the distance, he couldn't help but press his nose to the polymer windows, trying to view its cresting waves. Tristan leaned forward, placing his placing his arm around Phoenix and pointing out the sights.

"From this vantage point, you can see Paradrae Sea beyond the forest. Have you ever been there?"

"No, but I've heard it's lovely."

"The ascension of the twin moons is truly magical when viewed from the shore. Someday, we'll watch it together."

"I think I would like that," Phoenix said, knowing the likelihood of it happening was rather remote. Still, he wondered what it would be like, lying on the beach with Tristan as the waves lapped the shore and the moons reflected off the sea.

"To the south, hidden among the trees, lies Divinity Hamlet. It's populated mostly by heteros, and is said to be the birthplace of the Divinity's chosen — heteros, mascs and femmes."

"Yes, I remember my prelate teaching us the hamlet was where mascs were deemed the chosen."

"It's a good thing your sex appeal outshines your stubbornness," Tristan said, as he pressed a kiss below Phoenix's ear.

Phoenix shivered at the caress, wondering what Tristan meant. He wasn't stubborn — he was pragmatic.

"Over there, beneath the canopy of trees, are the Outlyers."

"Ah, yes. The hunters and gatherers. I don't understand their resistance to modernization."

"They're part of your constituency, love, and they're happy. Besides, they provide a valuable product to the depositories. The aromatics."

Phoenix shuddered at the mention of the aromatics. It would be a long time before the thought of cinfree didn't cause him to break into a sweat. Still, he listened as Tristan spoke of their plights. He made a mental note to assign an advisor to meet with the Outlyer leadership. Tristan's cry interrupted his thoughts and he gladly turned them away from the politics to the village below.

"Look, Phoenix. We're coming to Canopia." As the transport circled the colorful town, waiting for an opening to land at the ground level platform, Phoenix glanced to where Tristan pointed. Below them were tidy farms, their crops ripening under the bright Gemin sun. Children played in the meadow, many of them gathering flowers. The homes were quaint with dense thatched roofs and lovely pastel-hued walls, giving the village a fairytale ambiance.

With their neat, trimmed lawns and flower-lined walks, they looked like the houses depicted in the books he'd browsed through as a child. A long-forgotten memory of him staring in wonder at a pretty farm like these sparked to life. He'd sat with an old tome in his lap, ghosting his fingers over the yellowed pages, wishing he lived in a beautiful place like those pictured in the book. His parent had discovered him and had admonished Phoenix for daydreaming rather than studying the holovids of Prefecture Staquo government. Phoenix had grown up in a cold world of polymer and chrome with few embellishments, like holo-screens playing peaceful sea waves, or aviaries with colorful birds and greenery unlike any seen in Segratia.

"You're very fortunate to have known a place like Canopia," said Phoenix as he leaned back into his seat for the transport's descent. "From what I can see from here, the village seems to be a nurturing environment for a child."

"You're right. I can't tell you how much I loved living in Canopia. My childhood was unorthodox compared to others I grew up with."

"How so?"

"I had not only Loren and Riley, but also the input of my mother and a secondary father. With so many caring adults, I was kept busy and over-indulged. Some might say, 'spoiled.'"

"My own childhood was spent with one parent, much of it accompanying him to the incubation and emergent centers. From what I recall, if I wasn't with him making rounds, then I was in the holo-braries studying."

"What about playing and doing things for fun?"

"Well, there were some wonderful moments spent with the Arch Prelate. He was kind and nurturing."

"Your childhood sounds lonely compared with mine." Tristan kissed Phoenix on the cheek and held his hand.

"Please don't pity me."

"I don't, love. I admire you. Your upbringing has instilled a self-discipline that will serve you well as our mayor."

"Thank you. I hope you are right."

"Don't thank me yet. I intend to do all I can to unravel your self-control. Tonight, we'll share a bed beneath the twin moons and you will shout my name into the night while I do naughty things to your sweet ass."

Phoenix was still blushing at the images Tristan showed him when they stepped out of the transport and onto the platform where Riley and Loren waited. The two femmes were resplendent in their pastel pantaloons and bedazzling shirts. They wore leather sandals, showing off their colorful painted toenails.

"I'm so happy to see you, darlings. Loren says you're planning to stay with us for seven auroras. How exciting!"

"I'm sorry, Riley. I can spare just three auroras. I wish there could be more, but if I'm to step into the mayoral position, there are things which require my attention in Segratia."

"Darling, we will take whatever you can give us," said Loren with a flick of his wrist. He gazed lovingly at Tristan and hugged him before turning to Phoenix and giving him a heartfelt welcome.

"Come along, we're eager to show off our son and his gorgeous partner."

Carrying their portmanteaus, Tristan and Phoenix followed the femmes as they strutted through the main thoroughfare toward their small cottage. Phoenix tried to ignore the crowd they were attracting, but Tristan's reassurances through their psychic link encouraged him to smile and greet his constituents.

"After all, love, you will be governing the entire prefecture, not only Segratia and Hybridia."

With Tristan's words supporting him, he smiled and waved, taking a moment here and there to stop and talk with the children or listen to a gathering of farmers. Out of the corner of his eye, he spotted Terra Gaia and Wiccan Tall, whose sharp whistle caught his attention. Terra gave him a stern look and small smile, making him wonder why they weren't greeting him and their son.

"Mother and Wiccan will come by tonight to pay their respects," Tristan said. Phoenix tipped his head to the couple, acknowledging that he had seen them. The short walk to Tristan's parents' home took longer than normal because word of Phoenix's presence had circulated through the village with lightspeed. He was besieged by people wanting a moment or children begging to touch his gossamer hair. The previous mayors had never ventured into the Outlying area, and the villagers were excited to receive the soon-to-be mayor.

"Excuse us. Please, allow our guest to pass. Phoenix Ashe can make time for you tomorrow. For now, let our son's partner relax and enjoy his visit," Loren addressed the crowd, encouraging Tristan to keep walking with Phoenix.

Phoenix noticed the Canopians' visible disappointment as they dispersed. "Thank you for the warm greetings, everyone. I look forward to spending more time with you."

The spontaneous reception he'd received surprised and humbled Phoenix. He'd never expected the villagers to recognize him as their soon-to-be leader. He'd thought he and Tristan would arrive with no one taking notice, and he could enjoy his holiday in anonymity. Now he was committed to convening with his constituents on the morrow. Despite his insecurities, he looked forward to meeting with the people. He had noticed Canopia was home to a diverse population. He'd seen mascs, femmes and heteros. Not only were there couples of mixed singularities, there were children and elders, and impregnated women. He anticipated visiting and learning about all of them.

"Here we are, darlings. This is it, our humble abode," Riley said, sweeping his arms outward and smiling with pride at the tidy cottage and its beds of assorted flowers. Sparkling, opened windows boasted soft curtains billowing in the breeze. The ibis-egg blue walls held up a newly thatched roof. The warm yellow straw glowed from the sunlight piercing the dappling shadows from the trees' canopy. From the branches, songbirds welcomed him as much as the townspeople had. Phoenix shook his head, believing the quaint village was turning him into a romantic.

If I feel this way after an hour in town, what will happen at the end of my stay?

"Come, love. Let's go inside where it's cool."

"Please, help yourself to anything you would like. There are libations in the larder. Loren mixed them fresh this morning," Riley said, disappearing with their portmanteaus.

"Do you want a small nourishment before dinner?" Loren asked, leading Phoenix into the preparation area. Unlike Tristan's tiny cubicle, the femme's food-prep room was large enough to hold a wood hewn table with seating for eight.

He looked around the area, surprised to see the most modern of conveniences, including a robo-servant charging in the corner. From the picture window against one wall, he spied fields of crops growing in the hills beyond the cottage. Loren busied himself pouring libations and setting out a small feast to hold them over until the evening meal.

"I have put your bags in the larger room, loves. But I fear Phoenix will take up most of the space. The cubicle wasn't intended to accommodate a masc of your massive size," Riley said, coming in through the door. Phoenix blushed as Tristan's pretty parent ogled him.

"They'll be fine, my love. Tris mentioned they're going into the forest tonight, so as not to miss the last of the twin moons."

"Oh! It promises to be a beautiful night for a campout," Loren said, giving his son a lascivious, if not envious wink. "Tell me, Phoenix. What do you think of our little village?"

"It's certainly more than I expected, and the people are so friendly," he said. Ever the politician, he added, "I look forward to meeting with them and hearing their concerns. I'm glad you have arranged the opportunity for us to meet."

"Well, if anything the meet and greet will be impromptu. I warn you, Canopians can be very exuberant both in their pleasure and displeasure."

"I understand, but I don't know that I have done anything to provoke them. It's not like I've been in office or had any influence over the previous administration."

"Darling, you're so naïve. You are guilty by association. You're 'the man' and the villagers dislike 'the man'. I'm just warning you that despite their welcome today, they will want answers to questions you haven't yet considered."

Loren requested Riley's help with something in the bedroom, cutting the dire warning short. Shrugging, Riley followed his partner, grumbling about Loren's inopportune timing.

"What is so important he couldn't have waited?" Phoenix asked before popping another tidbit into his mouth.

"Oh, love. Riley is right. You're very naïve. Loren dragged him away to save you from more discourse on Canopian and Segratian politics. There's nothing Riley likes more than a good political debate."

"Loren didn't have to do that. I don't mind indulging your parent."

"Trust me, you'll get your fill during the morrow's meet and greet."

They spent the rest of the afternoon talking with Riley and Loren about their crops and the shop. Tristan's parents agreed that Terra's banishment had set her on a course of unstoppable creativity which was sure to profit them all. They were sharing a laugh at her expense when she shouted from the yard.

"I can hear you!"

"Mother!" Tristan jumped up to greet Terra and Wiccan, hugging her fiercely before releasing her and striking his secondary father soundly on the back.

"Wiccan, Terra. It's nice to see you once again," Phoenix said, shaking the tall hetero's hand before hugging Terra.

"Tris. Phoenix. I'm glad you decided to visit," Wiccan said, nudging his wife.

"Yes, it is good to see you—both of you."

"Mother, don't you have something to say to Phoenix?"

With a big and over-loud sigh, Terra said, "I'm very sorry for my indiscretion last time we met. I insulted my son, and I placed the fault at your feet. I hope you can find it within yourself to forgive me."

Tristan smiled at his mother, proud of her for humbling herself before Phoenix. She could be gracious when she chose. Her rapier tongue often got her in trouble with his parents and Wiccan as well.

"Thank you, Terra Gaia. Your apology is accepted and the indiscretion forgotten. Come join us for libations."

"Where are Loren and Riley?" Wiccan asked.

"They're out in the fields harvesting the vegetables for dinner. Loren insisted on vine-fresh."

"Well, in that case, I'll join them, if you don't mind."

"Not at all. They'll appreciate the help," Tristan said.

"Would you join me, Phoenix? I'm certain Tris' parents are eager to show you their farm."

Phoenix glanced at Tristan, who nodded. Phoenix's absence would give him the opportunity to inform his mother about the meeting on the morrow without distressing his lover. With one last glance over his shoulder, Phoenix followed Wiccan out of the door, listening to him explain the benefits of growing the crops on the hills.

"That was a very nice apology, Mother. I'm proud of you."

"You don't think I poured the contriteness on too thick?"

"No. You sounded sincere, even though I'm sure it pained you to do so."

"You don't give me enough credit. I meant what I said and I'm sorry I insinuated you are a whore. However, I am so very happy you're no longer working in that dreadful establishment. You have much more to offer the world than your attendant skills, which I don't even want to think about. Now tell me, what do you and Phoenix have planned for your stay?"

Chapter Fifteen

Tristan spread a polymer tarp over the soft, damp meadow grass. In the middle, he placed a folded packet and inserted a tiny capsule into its center, asking Phoenix to stand back. With a hiss, the envelope expanded until sitting on the covering was a king-sized mattress with a silver reflective blanket.

Tristan looked to Phoenix and said, "The nights in the forest can become cold, but we won't have to worry about our comfort. Come, let's get naked and I'll show you all the cool stuff the celestial skies have that you don't see in the city."

"Umm, can't you show me the 'cool stuff' if I'm wearing my clothes?"

"I suppose. But, where's the fun in that?" Tristan replied with a pout. "Besides, isn't it better if I tug your nipple rings while pointing out the twin moonrise? The constellation Mastodon Minor is never brighter than with a hungry cock tickling your pleasure gland."

Phoenix arched his eyebrow and crossed his arms over his chest. "And you know this how?"

"Or so I've been told." Tristan hastened to answer with a teasing wink and grin.

Phoenix longed for what Tristan offered him, but was hesitant being out in the open. What if someone happened upon them fucking in the woods? The scandal in the prefecture would rival that of the outgoing mayor. Uncertain about removing his clothing, he gaped at Tristan, who had divested himself of his clothes and was lying back on the mattress, stroking his cock and leering at him. His boldness tempted Phoenix to shout "fuck caution" and join him.

Mesmerized by the tantalizing picture Tristan made, Phoenix licked his bottom lip and tossed shirt and pantaloons into the thicket, yelling, "Fuck convention!"

"That's the spirit, love."

Phoenix settled next to his lover and pulled him in for a hungry kiss, biting and probing his lips with teeth and tongue. They made out under the stars until Tristan tore away from their embrace. His breath came quick and hard, as if he'd run all the way to Canopia from Segratia.

"Phoenix, my love, as enticing as you are, I want to show you the moonrise, and it's rapidly approaching."

"Hmm. Come back here."

"Tempting, but no. Open your eyes."

"Oh! Isn't that gorgeous?" Phoenix stared past Tristan, noting the luminosity on the horizon as the moons began their ascent. He'd seen the twins rise before, many times, but the city lights dimmed much of the spectacle. The meadow's clearing gave them a wondrous view as the orbs climbed into the sky. Phoenix had never experienced the pale violet glow of the coronas. The sight of them rising above the hill mesmerized him. When he'd observed them from his pinnacle, the planetoids were an uninteresting blotched gray. The poets waxed on about the glorious illumination, but Phoenix hadn't understood the attraction for the shining globes until now.

As promised, Tristan tugged his nipple rings, eliciting a groan and returning his attention to the alluring femme. He smiled at the tender expression Tristan wore. When Tristan cupped his cheek and sent Phoenix a message expressing his joy at being able to share this moment with him, Phoenix leaned in, claiming Tristan's lips in a heated kiss.

Moonrise forgotten, he took his time, savoring the texture of the Tristan's mouth and the velvety glide of his lover's tongue on his own. Slow and easy, Tristan slid his tongue along his, swallowing his lusty moans. When kissing wasn't enough, Tristan turned until he'd positioned himself head to foot with Phoenix. Unable to resist the temptation of Tristan's engorged shaft, he took it between his lips and fellated him until Tristan's groans matched his own. When Tristan swallowed his cock, Phoenix thought he'd die from the heart-stopping pleasure. He relished Tristan's pre-seminal fluids coating his throat. Tristan hummed each time Phoenix groaned. Then he cried out whenever Phoenix swallowed, taking him deep into his throat.

Grasping and writhing, sweat pouring off his body, he laved Tristan's hard shaft with relish, wanting him to come first. But Tristan's skill exceeded his own and soon Phoenix was ready to beg.

"You're killing me," Phoenix thought, hoping Tristan was reading his musings. He struggled to hold on to the orgasm that was just out of reach, knowing Tristan was playing his body like a finely tuned instrument. He

giggled when he realized he was in love with a cock maestro.

Wait! What?

"It's too late. You can't take it back," Phoenix heard Tristan through their psychic link.

"Take what back?" he mumbled around a very aroused and leaking cock, forgetting he didn't need to use his voice. Tristan was reading his mind.

"You called me a cock maestro," Tristan messaged.

Phoenix was relieved Tristan had ignored his admittance of love. Perhaps, if he was lucky, he hadn't heard him. Besides, confessions of love in the throes of passion were unreliable. Phoenix was certain Tristan had heard hundreds over the spans.

"You flatter me, love."

Unable to answer, because his mouth was full and his mind was concentrating on withholding his impending orgasm, Phoenix swallowed, humming with satisfaction when his lover clasped him tight and undulated his hips. He wanted Tristan to let go, to fill him with his cum, and to shout his name to the Divinity in ecstasy. The empowerment he received from bringing Tristan to fulfillment was unlike anything Phoenix had experienced in his thirty spans. The gorgeous femme completed him.

Tristan trembled and groaned beneath him. He could no longer contain Tristan's shaft as his own passion overwhelmed him. With a pop, he released his zealous lover and pumped his hips, fucking Tristan's mouth. His cock thickened as his seminal fluids spilled. Before he'd caught his breath, Phoenix returned to sucking Tristan with abandon, desperate to bring him the same gratifying release.

"Oh, glorious Divinity! Phoenix!" Tristan's cries echoed through the forest, startling the small animals in the undergrowth. Despite Tristan's shouts, Phoenix heard their scampering and rustling as they sought quieter fields. Phoenix hollowed his cheeks and sucked Tristan dry, swallowing his spend with relish. "Enough, love," Tristan said. Phoenix kept sucking, hoping to extract another orgasm from his lover. "I can't. Your loving ministrations have rendered me incapable." Phoenix couldn't contain his self-satisfied grin.

Tristan rolled away from Phoenix, catching his breath and listening to his heart's frantic beating. The masc's skill had pulled the orgasm from him as if Phoenix rather than Tristan had spent the last few spans working the depositories. Tristan's body hummed with his fulfillment. Beside him Phoenix lay on his back, his meaty cock still engorged and leaking. The pre-seminal fluids puddled in the furrows of his muscular abdomen, glistening beneath the moonlight and sparkling against his deep plum complexion.

Unable to help himself, Tristan ran a finger through the viscous liquid and painted his lips with the secretions. Tristan turned around and faced Phoenix, encouraging the masc to taste himself in his kiss. He wrapped his fingers in Phoenix's hair and plundered his mouth, loving the flavor of his passion. He trailed his kisses lower, licking and biting the heated flesh. When he reached Phoenix's nipple, he tugged the ring with his teeth and pulled on the other. Tristan wished he could see him wearing his nipple chain. The sight of Phoenix wearing his aqua pendant hanging from the delicate links during the display parade had given him immense pleasure.

Lost in carnal ecstasy, Phoenix writhed and moaned with each drag on his sensitized nubs. Tristan licked his way to the small divot hiding between rippled abs and lapped the fluids pooled there. He followed the trail of fine silvery hair to the nest of curls adorning Phoenix's tantalizing near-black cock. He inhaled, loving the scent of his partner's sensuality. Lust and need and Phoenix's own unique musk engulfed him. He tongued the sacs and one by one sucked them into his mouth, laving them until Phoenix could no longer lie passive.

The masc spread his legs and lifted his knees, holding them to give Tristan easy access to his opening. He whimpered, but Tristan ignored his invitation and continued paying homage to his alluring ball sac. He squirmed, wiggling his ass, tempting Tristan to pay attention to his quivering entrance. He laughed, certain Phoenix heard the wry chuckle in his thoughts and realized Tristan knew exactly what he was doing to him.

"Dammit, Tristan. Fuck me!" he demanded, sounding frustrated and overloud in the quiet forest.

"I would comply, my love, but your oral skills have left me...umm...well, deflated. Give me a few moments and I will gladly succumb to your charms once more." Tristan continued paying homage to Phoenix's sacs, sucking and lapping the tender pouches.

"Your tongue. Use your mouth, your fingers, anything. Just fuck me!"

And he did. Tristan penetrated his demanding lover's channel with one finger, but not enough for Phoenix to achieve the climax he craved. With the expertise he'd mastered as a premier attendant, Tristan edged his partner, appreciating his entreaties to please, please, please, give him his orgasm. With his begging ringing in his ears, it didn't take long until his own cock had hardened again, and Tristan was set to pound his lover into their makeshift mattress under the stars.

Tristan glanced upward and spied the constellation he sought. "I'm ready, love. Put yourself on your hands and knees."

Phoenix didn't move and position himself until Tristan asked a second time. The sight of Phoenix's perfect body trembling as he lifted himself and held the submissive position inflamed Tristan beyond measure. His heart pounded and his body vibrated with ravenous need as he prepared Phoenix. His channel walls pulsated as Tristan stretched him using two then three fingers, spreading the lubricant along his insatiable passage.

"Please, Tristan. I need you."

Tristan entered his lover with interminable slowness, stopping to savor the intoxicating warmth surrounding his hard shaft. These were the moments that drove him near senseless when the urge to fuck wrestled with the desire to give his partner life's ultimate pleasure. He ran his hand over Phoenix's back as he watched the black-orchid body swallowing his cock and driving him close to insane with the need to spill his seminal fluids into the welcoming heat. Phoenix's diamond-dusted skin glistened in the twin moonlight, highlighting the furrows and ripples of his powerful muscles.

Tristan wrapped one arm around Phoenix and hooked the other under his arm, lifting him to his knees and plastering him to his chest. He brushed the strands of hair from his sweat-dampened face and bit his jaw, licking the thick tendon beneath, following it to the sweet spot where shoulders and neck joined. Phoenix growled when Tristan nipped him again and lapped away the sting.

"Look up, love." Tristan coaxed Phoenix's head upward with a slight tug on his hair. "Open your eyes. What do you see?"

"The moons are higher in the sky. It's too dark to see much else. Enough stargazing. Fuck me."

"Is that all you want?"

"Fuck yes! No. Yes. No, I want more. But for now, I'd settle for a kiss."

Tristan chuckled. "I'm glad you clarified that for me. Kissing is a good place to start."

Phoenix turned his head, and Tristan took advantage of his offering. Their lips met and Tristan began a slow glide in and out of Phoenix's channel. With each inward push, Phoenix groaned and shuddered, testing Tristan's control over his own need to orgasm.

"Open your eyes, love. Tell me what you see."

"Stars. There are so many stars. The moons' coronas glow pale lavender…much like your skin. Oh, you feel sooo fucking good."

Tristan smiled and brushed his cock against his lover's pleasure gland. "Do you see the six-point cluster just above the horizon and below the moons?" Phoenix nodded, and Tristan hit his gland again. He increased his tempo and kept rocking against that pleasure-charged bundle of nerves, keeping Phoenix from speaking. "That's the Mastodon Minor constellation. Keep your eyes on it and don't look away no matter how much you might want to."

"M'kay." Phoenix leaned his head back on Tristan's shoulder but kept his gaze on the stars.

Tristan kissed his temple and fucked Phoenix with a steady rhythm. He tugged his nipple rings each time his cock bumped the sensitive bundle of nerves, savoring each drawn-out moan of his aroused partner. Phoenix vibrated in his arms as his climax approached, but he kept his gaze locked on the heavens while Tristan couldn't stop watching the ecstatic expression on his lover's face.

Around them the breeze ceased to blow. Insects quieted until the only sound in the night was the *slap slap* of skin on skin. Phoenix stared at the Mastodon constellation, marveling at its clarity. Without Segratia's lights hampering his view, the arrangement of stars that made up the fabled constellation shimmered with magical brilliance. Mesmerized, Phoenix was certain he imagined the beast coming to life. He strained to get a better look, but something restrained him. He quivered with the compulsion to succumb to the call of the wild creature. White heat suffused his blood and every muscle tensed with insatiable need.

"Yes, my love. I've got you… always. Let yourself go. I'm here to catch you."

"Tristan?"

"Phoenix, darling. You're almost there. Come, love, and join me."

"Oh Divinity. Tristan!"

Phoenix's entire being spasmed around the thick cock filling him. His ecstatic cries rang out as he transcended. Orgasm without ejaculation in the arms of his treasured lover. *How have I never known of the Divinity's most precious gift to her children?*

"Because, my love, transcendence only happens when the parties are involved and committed body, mind and soul. Within the femme culture, experiencing the sacred joining forms a lifelong commitment to one another. A marriage, so to speak."

Chapter Sixteen

Phoenix stood in the middle of the village meeting house, greeting his constituents. His body was sore from his night of roughing it and his mind was in a turmoil since he had discovered he'd unknowingly made a permanent promise to Tristan. His anger boiled beneath the surface. The femme should have told him the significance of their hot tub fuck the first time they had 'transcended'.

Phoenix smiled and shook hands and struggled to pay attention to what the villagers said to him. He put on his best politician face while he replayed last night's campout debacle in his head. After his post-transcendence euphoria had dissipated, comprehension had smacked Phoenix hard.

He had seethed while Tristan explained the extraordinary experience had bonded them. Tristan had tried explaining that was the reason finding him with Gareth had made Phoenix so livid. Their connection was secured and they were mated for life.

Tristan was telling him they were bonded, destined to live their lives together. No way. He was a masc…the prime masc of Segratia. He intended for his life partner to be masc. There was no possibility the femme could be right. A vivid picture of Tristan on his knees, fellating Gareth stoked his anger.

'Fuck you, Tristan! If that were true, and we were bonded, I wouldn't have found you with Gareth's cock stuffed down your throat. A proper partner doesn't service his mate's best friend!' Phoenix realized there was something wrong with his logic, but he was too fucking angry to give a damn.

'Phoenix, love – '

'Don't 'Phoenix, love' me. I'm not allowing you to manipulate me any longer,' he yelled, stumbling about searching for his clothes in the dark clearing. He slipped into his pantaloons and stepped into his shoes before stomping off into the forest to vent his frustration and outrage.

'Come back, Phoenix. You'll lose your way without enough light to see.'

'Get out of my fucking head!' Phoenix roared.

Phoenix marched on, not caring where he went and ignoring Tristan's pleas for him to return. He stumbled to his knees and scraped his palms on the brambles beneath him. He breathing was labored and though his initial ire had faded, his rapid heartbeat and irritability continued. It was then he realized his cock was still erect and begging for release. Transcendence had done nothing for his raging hard-on.

"Let me take care of you, love. Come back and I'll suck you until you cry out for the Divinity's blessing."

Phoenix ripped open his codpiece and gripped his shaft, tugging and squeezing until his orgasm was upon him. 'Fuck you, Tristan!' he shouted to the heavens as streams of ejaculate landed on a nearby tree. When he finished, he kept walking, ignoring his spirit's dissatisfaction and Tristan's pleas and promises to make things right, if he would only return.

He wandered for hours, stopping to rest near a burbling brook. The water's soothing sound eventually lulled him to sleep. At day break he awoke to Tristan's voice calling his name. He opened his eyes in confusion at his whereabouts. Though he didn't say anything, Phoenix sensed the femme in his thoughts, guiding him until he came upon Canopia. With nowhere else to go, he made his way to Riley's and Loren's cottage.

Their sad faces told him they knew what had happened. He had rejected their son as his life's partner. He thought he should apologize, but couldn't come up with the right words to convey his anger, confusion and regret. Even though Tristan had deceived him, he acknowledged their connection and recognized the lonely discontent within his soul.

"Good morrow, darling," Riley greeted him with a hug. "There's a restorative libation waiting for you on the food-prep counter."

Phoenix glanced around, fearing Tristan's inevitable arrival. "Don't worry. He's not here." At Phoenix's surprised gasp, Loren explained the femme's absence. "Once Tris knew you were almost home, he refused to cause you any discomfort, so he caught a transport."

"Where did he go?"

"He didn't say, love. Just grabbed his portmanteau and disappeared out the door."

"All right, Phoenix Ashe. How will you fix it?" a grizzled voice interrupted his reverie.

"I'm sorry?" Phoenix shook his head and admonished himself for letting Tristan interfere with his meet and greet. Standing before him was an older man, a hetero who looked disappointed. Next to him stood a pretty femme with his eyes downcast.

"Just like I told you, Pasquale. He don't care, any more than the last mayorfucker."

"No. It's not that I'm not sympathetic to your plight, it's that I didn't quite get all the nuances of what you were saying," Phoenix said, congratulating himself for his quick-thinking reply.

"Nice save." Terra's lyrical voice filled his head. He glanced over his shoulder and saw her and Wiccan leaning against a wall, watching him. *"But if you can't keep your thoughts under control, Willis and his partner, Pasquale, are going to realize you're not listening. They'll believe the rumor which say you don't mind that the government won't allow them to marry."*

"Why can't they marry?"

"Willis is hetero, or rather hybrid. After his wife passed over to the Divinity's care, he met and fell in love with Pasquale."

"But Pasquale is femme!"

"Your point?"

"He can only wed another femme."

"But they've transcended and are bonded. What are they to do if you don't morally sanction their marriage?"

"Excuse me," Willis interrupted their psychic conversation. "I just thought you should know my Pasquale is an accomplished telepath. And for that matter, so am I. We met at the Center of Telepathic Expansion, where Pasqual teaches."

Phoenix raised his eyebrows and had the good grace to stammer out his apology before reassuring the striking couple. Once he became mayor, he would speak with his advisors about their wish to marry. He promised to return to Canopia and discuss their recommendations.

"Hmpf. Sounds like a lot of empty promises to me," Willis grumbled, taking Pasquale's arm and leading him to a vacant seat.

"May I get your attention?" Wiccan's booming voice bounced off the walls of the meeting room, which also served as the dance hall for the attached tavern. The room was filled with an assortment of people. Femmes, mascs, heteros, singular couples, mixed partners, and even more dyads like Willis and Pasquale took up the seats and stood together in the back of the room.

Phoenix's eyes widened at the number of singular women in the audience. In one corner, a group of surly adolescents stared at him with animosity. He was unaccustomed to womankind and youthful citizens. Segratia was a purlieu of mascs. Except for the occasional hetero, Hybridia was filled with femmes. Singular women…sapphics…were a rarity in Segratian society.

Phoenix strode up the four stage steps to the makeshift podium Wiccan had put together. He heard the gasps from the assembly and wondered why they viewed him as an enigma. He was masc…not so unusual. Riley and Loren gave him encouraging smiles as he peered out into the crowd. He fingered the pendant around his neck and gathered a small measure of confidence from its presence. Terra's knowing look he didn't understand, until he realized he was still wearing Tristan's pendant. He turned it loose and grasped the podium sides before he began speaking.

"Good morningtide. First off, I want to thank Loren and Riley Faire for hosting me. Their generosity makes it possible to be here with you today." Phoenix nodded his greeting and mouthed a thank you to his hosts.

The two femmes surprised him by giggling. However, through a psychic connection Riley said, *"You are most welcome, darling."*

One of these times I'll remember I am dealing with a group of extraordinary telepaths.

"I also want to express my appreciation to Terra Gaia and Wiccan Tall for encouraging me to visit your lovely village. The beauty and bounty of Canopia is a treasured source of pride to the prefecture."

"Keep your remarks true, Phoenix," Terra cautioned. *"These people are here because Segratia has neglected their existence and they want to know how you will remedy the oversight."*

Phoenix scanned the faces of the eclectic assembly. They didn't appear too friendly, so he decided to heed Terra's warning.

"I can't speak for the earlier administration, but I offer you these guarantees. I've heard your concerns and I understand your plights. Discrimination and indifference have too long been the attitudes by which the prefecture was governed.

"Mascs want their love for their femme partners to be recognized as true. Heteros are asking us not to discriminate against them for being emerged as the Divinity designed. Femmes, I feel your plight more than you know. You're in danger of becoming extinct without low-cost, easy access to the incubation chambers. Hetero couples want the same opportunities as the Segratian and Hybridian citizens, to own property and education for their children. To the sapphics and hybrids, I say it's time to come out of the shadows and stomp discrimination to the ground. We are all a reflection of the Divinity, and I have begun to learn her image is fluid. I apologize for not recognizing this truth sooner.

"The youth," Phoenix continued, glancing toward the adolescents who occupied themselves with their technology, "want to know that there are opportunities available to them, more than those predestined in their genealogy." The testy juveniles snapped their heads upward from the holo-phones in their hands, suddenly paying attention. "Don't look so surprised, my friends. It wasn't all that long ago I was your age. I harbored dreams of sailing the Paradrae Sea and becoming a merchant. However, my parent made certain I honored my engineered DNA commitment. I was meant to govern Prefecture Staquo, which I will to the best of my ability. Besides, I've discovered telepaths make better merchants than an oversized, self-absorbed physician's son."

There was a spattering of laughter around the room. The juveniles nodded and returned to their holo-phones and pads. Phoenix rubbed the pendant at his throat and wondered where Tristan had withdrawn to. He spotted Terra watching his fingers as he rubbed the gem. She winked at him and grinned. He turned his attention back to his audience, leaving him to wonder about her strange reaction. He coughed once and began his remarks.

"After meeting all of you, and experiencing other recent events, I'm beginning to understand a few things. The Divinity intended me to be your mayor. The mystery of the why has started to unfold. There are changes on the horizons and difficulties in the breeze. But when the clouds part, we will emerge a stronger, more unified prefecture. So, I humbly ask you for patience, your faith and the opportunity to answer your demands. Thank you."

Wiccan joined Phoenix and patted him on the back. "Well done. You are a work in progress, but you will make a fine mayor. Thank you for meeting with us."

"You are most welcome."

"Fellow Canopians. Our next mayor, Phoenix Ashe." Wiccan's voice rang out across the hall as he walked with Phoenix to the end of the stage. The crowd responded with enthusiastic applause, a little skepticism and polite smiles. It was a start.

Phoenix and Wiccan made their way to Terra, who stood chatting with Loren and Riley.

"Well done, son," Loren said, giving his shoulder a quick squeeze.

"Darling, you were superb. I only regret that Tris — " Loren poked Riley before he could express his regrets and dragged him off to visit with a gathering of sapphic couples. Phoenix didn't pay much attention to Terra as she shared her opinions of his talk. His mind kept wondering to Tris as he fingered the pendant.

"Enjoyed your speech, Mr. Mayor sir," said one of the adolescents who approached him. He was femme, with a delicate build and no taller than Terra Gaia. Phoenix wondered if he'd ever fill out with muscles or reach Tristan's height.

"Thank you, uh… What's your name?"

"Pense Petuniason, sir. But my friends call me Pensie."

"Well, Pensie. I'm very pleased to meet you."

"Is it true, sir?"

"Is what true?"

"That you and Tris have transcended and bonded?"

"What? How do you know?"

"Pense Petuniason! One simply does not ask their mayor questions about his transcendence in public. Or ever. Despite what you and your friends think, there are some matters meant to remain private." Terra's outrage was palpable as she admonished the youthful femme, shaking her finger in his face and causing his complexion to pale.

"But, everyone already knows. Just look. I mean he's *wearing* Tristan's pendant and gems, so everybody can see for themselves he's taken." In true adolescent form, the young femme rolled his eyes.

"Please explain how you came to this conclusion?" Phoenix asked, fearful he was aware of the answer before Pense could offer an explanation.

"That you and Tristan are life partners?" Phoenix nodded and scowled. "The jewel matches his cerulean eyes, and the Divinity teaches us that only the chosen one shall wear the rare colored stone."

What? Why have I never heard of this so-called prophecy? Masc for masc and femme for femme. Those are the teachings of the Divinity. "You must be mistaken. It is nothing but an adornment." Phoenix didn't care for the skeptical look Pense directed his way, nor the giggles of the other young femmes.

Chapter Seventeen

Phoenix stared out at Segratia from his pinnacle apartment. The sun had set hours ago, leaving melancholy in its wake. The twins were high in the heavens, looking drab and nothing like the amethyst glowing orbs he'd experienced while lying with Tristan. Without him, their magic had dimmed. Tonight, they were round humongous gray rocks mockingly reflecting the sun's light back onto the prefecture.

Seven auroras had passed since Phoenix had departed Canopia to return home. He had stayed with Loren and Riley for the three promised auroras before coming back to Segratia. Tristan had never returned, leaving him with plenty of time to visit with his hosts, and also Terra and Wiccan. Not only had he gotten to know them better, he'd heard tales of Tristan's childhood that were sure to embarrass the femme, if he had been there. What stood out most in Phoenix's mind was Tristan's unmatched telepathic abilities.

Terra had explained that most of the planet's populace were telepaths. But without constant use the skill waned until it disappeared. Her parents had nurtured her skills as a child and she had done the same with Tristan. He had surprised them all with his unprecedented proficiency, prompting her to make the trip daily to Hybridia's telepathic center, where she'd enrolled him.

'He was their prize pupil. The headmaster wanted him to mentor and eventually teach.'

'What happened? How did he end working in the depository?'

'When he went through his adolescent development, one thing we didn't expect was for his eyes to change color.'

'What? That's unheard of!'

'He was a beautiful, yellow-haired femme with sky-blue eyes. When he had finished growing and putting on muscle, they had transformed into the brilliant cerulean they are today. Many of the villagers thought he was demon-possessed, or they believed the change a portent of evil. Canopians he'd known all his life began rejecting or avoiding him.'

'How heartbreaking for him. But I don't understand why that brought him to the promenade.'

'Remember what adolescence was like...the raging hormones...the erections that never left you...the multiple orgasms,' Wiccan said with a euphoric expression and a chuckle.

Phoenix laughed, remembering well the frustrating days and nights with only his own touch for relief. 'You're saying, he worked in the depositories to satisfy his youthful libido.'

'Partly. The son of the Seminal Depository's director mentored at the center. He noticed Tristan during the graduation preparations and suggested he would make a superb attendant. He convinced him his unusual eye color *and exceptional telepathic skills would be the key to his success.'*

Phoenix was uncertain whether to affirm Tristan's accomplishments. After all, he was speaking with the femme's mother and secondary parent. Good sense told him a mother wouldn't want to know the fine points of her son's sexual prowess.

'You are wise to keep quiet, Phoenix Ashe. I know my son was considered the prime attendant of Hybridia and many sought his attentions. I'm also aware he saw to your inaugural deposit. There's no need for embarrassment. You are, for all intents, our son-in-canon. You only need the Prelate to sanctify your union.'

'I've been misled into a relationship I had no intent of pursuing. I like you and the rest of Tristan's family, but I can't remain bonded to him, nor will I ask for the Divinity's blessing.'

'You silly boy. Divine sanction has been yours since the moment you emerged from your incubation chamber. The ancient recordings have promised us someone of singularity to guide and meld the cultures of the prefecture into a cohesive society. The day Tristan's eyes turned cerulean, he began having visions of the one chosen for him by the Divinity. A formidable masc with diamond-dusted lavender skin reminiscent of the twin moons' celestial glow.'

'You're mistaken. Neither of us are all that special. I'm genetically predisposed to govern, and I am plagued with doubts about my ability to do so. Tristan…sure, he's a talented telepath and an exceptional depository attendant, but there are others with the same skills. You're wrong about the Divinity's intentions.'

'No, Phoenix Ashe. It is you who is misguided. Qandi Kane tried telling you of your unusual connection to my son. Only your obstinacy – '

High up in his apartment, Phoenix shook his head at the memory. He'd been mortified that Qandi had shared their inebriated ramblings and conversation with Tristan's mother. Shortly after he'd finished shaking hands with the villagers, he'd called for a ground transport and departed for Segratia. Within the small confines of his transport cabin, he hadn't been able to escape thoughts of Tristan. He smelled him on his clothes and skin.

Even after arriving home, Tristan plagued him. He heard his lusty moans and promises of love in his mind. He held his hands over his ears to shut out the unwanted sounds, but it did no good. Certain the femme was using telepathy on him, he shouted out for him to get out of his head. But he knew the voices weren't put there artificially. They were memories…visions he didn't want to forget.

What have you done to me?

There was no answer. Silence reigned and loneliness was its complement. Defeated, acknowledging he couldn't stop thinking of Tristan no matter how hard he tried, Phoenix retired to his bed. Lying on the sheets where he and the femme had made love did little to induce sleep. Tristan's scent was everywhere, leaving Phoenix with no peace. Like he had the last six nights, Phoenix closed his eyes and dreamt of his lover and their romantic idyll beneath Gemin's moons.

He awoke with an erection hungry for Tristan's ministrations. Hot and hard, Phoenix needed relief. He clasped his cock and stroked it the way that always felt best. He opened a packet of lubricant and applied it to his erection after his slit refused to issue pre-seminal fluids. Phoenix fondled and tugged his shaft to the point of irritation as his frustration grew. He played with his ball sac, but his ache for a climax only increased. He reached for a phallus, much like the one he'd experienced in Tristan's tub—the one modeled after his lover.

Frustrated, he lubed the clear polymer and pressed it against heated entrance, gasping at its cold, hard, impersonal feel. He pushed, but his stubborn body refused its entrance. Near to tears with his need to come, Phoenix thought of his inaugural deposit and the sensuality of watching his seed jettison. He imagined Tristan tonguing him, but the visuals just fueled his dissatisfaction. He fucked his fist with a vengeance and still couldn't climax.

Perhaps with the heated lube his body would allow the phallus' penetration. He reached for the little-used lubricant and mistakenly grasped the choker with Tristan's pendant. He'd tossed it aside and forgotten about it once he'd returned home. Now the stone felt warm and alive in his hand. He stared at the glowing jewel and, uncaring about its significance, fastened the adornment around his neck. Warmth and peace suffused his exasperated body and heartsick soul.

Driven to satisfy his craving for release, he stroked his cock. At the renewed attention, pre-seminal fluid coated its length, negating the need for lubricant. Phoenix threw his head back, stretching his neck's tendons as his climax approached. "Fuck!" he shouted as streams of aqua-tinted cum erupted, coating his hand and landing on his chest. He rubbed the warm, grape-scented essence into his skin, thinking of the times Tristan had done the same. Phoenix missed those intimate moments…the tender ones when the need to touch and kiss outweighed the need to orgasm.

He ran a finger along the pendant, noticing that it hummed against his skin. He wondered if Tristan thought of him and half-expected to hear him answer.

Phoenix dozed with silence ringing in his ears.

When he next awakened, he realized he hadn't much time until he was scheduled to meet with the Segratia's Arch Prelate, his old friend Thom Didymas. He listened for Tristan and was met with nothing. The femme's absence was becoming his constant companion. Phoenix didn't like it. He showered, dressed and partook of a small repast before his ground transport arrived.

The tall, imposing spires of the cathedral were the first thing he saw as the conveyance rounded the byway's corner, narrowly missing a slow-footed pedestrian. Before alighting, he sent a message to the maintenance department to have the unit's motion detectors tested. It wouldn't do to have the mayor's ride strike a constituent.

Phoenix glanced up at the grandiose building with its stained polymer windows and alabaster walls. At night, the cathedral reflected the violet glow of the moons, but during the day, it shone bright white. Phoenix followed a narrow walkway around the church, which led to the prelate's quarters. It was where his old friend, the Arch Prelate, would be reading. The masc had been his spiritual and moral counselor for as long as he remembered.

"Good day, Phoenix Ashe," the high prelate greeted him from the bench on which he sat reading beneath the ancient birch tree. He was wearing his customary robes. Pale lavender linen, secured at the waist with a twisted rope of black-orchid silk. The combination reminded him of Tristan. He shook his head to clear the unwanted memory. He couldn't face his confessor displaying an erection.

"Good afternoon, your Grace. I hope I haven't kept you waiting too long with my tardiness."

"Nonsense. You're right on time. Please join me." The elder ecclesiastic set aside his book and moved over to make room for Phoenix's large frame. "Now, tell me. What is on your mind? I sense you are troubled."

"You've always known when something was bothering me, and today is no different. The mayoral inauguration soon takes place, and I fear I'm not ready. I've come seeking your counsel."

"I have watched you grow from a small weed of a boy into the magnificent and reverent masc you have become. I've seen you weather things that would knock most of the Divinity's children off their collective feet. There has never been another more capable of governing our prefecture than you, Phoenix Ashe. It is, of course, the Divinity's will."

"How can you be sure?" Phoenix stared into the wizened face of the prelate and wondered when he had aged.

"What is going on with you? You have never questioned my word."

"I wish I knew, Thom. I'm so confused," Phoenix said, standing and pacing with frustration.

"Then, let's talk about it…inside, where it's cooler." Thom Didymas rose, leaning on Phoenix as they walked into the interior of the rectory. Once they were comfortably seated, and the housekeeper had seen to their needs, Phoenix began talking.

He shared with his prelate and friend the conversation he'd had with Terra Gaia the first day he'd met Tristan's formidable mother. It was that conversation which had first put doubts into his mind about his beliefs toward the Divinity. Thom spoke about faith and stressed there was no right or wrong way to worship the Divinity provided no living creature was harmed in the process. Terra Gaia intrigued him with her belief that Phoenix and Tristan were selected by the Divinity. He admitted that as a young seminarian, he had studied the ancient recordings, but had dismissed them in favor of more modern tenets.

"Perhaps I was hasty to do so. There is truth in the knowledge and prophecies of our ancestors. You cannot discount the possibility that a more cohesive society would be good for Gemin and our prefecture."

"So, you're saying Terra was right, and I am destined to partner with her son, Tristan Faire. Are we then to marry and establish a precedent for mixed couples? What about the others…sapphics and hybrids? They're making similar demands."

"The word of the Divinity teaches us that we reflect her grace. Nowhere does she teach us to differentiate between her children. Prejudice came from within Gemin's inhabitants — not from the Divinity."

"Why wasn't I taught this before?"

"You must forgive an old masc. I too have forgotten the teachings of the ancient ones and have been influenced by the previous administrators who benefitted by maintaining the status quo. When good fortune shone on them, the offering plates were full, and the church prospered."

Phoenix sat in silence, reflecting on what the prelate said. He wondered what his former teacher was thinking. The shameful expression he wore broke Phoenix's heart.

"Come with me to the cathedral and we will pray for the Divinity's guidance and forgiveness. Perhaps she will show this old fool how to make amends and do right by you."

Phoenix sat inside with his longtime friend and mentor, watching in stunned disbelief as the robed masc prostrated himself. He begged forgiveness for having tarnished the Divinity's teachings in exchange for ill-gotten mintage. When the prelate was satisfied with the Divinity's absolution, Phoenix helped him to rise and return to the rectory. With a carafe of libations at hand, they spoke long into the night of old times and Phoenix's upcoming inauguration.

Phoenix returned to his cold pinnacle apartment. Loneliness still resided in his heart, filling the space Tristan had vacated. He fingered the pendant which he couldn't bring himself to remove. The weight of the jewelry grounded him much as his visit with the prelate had eliminated his confusion.

He located his holo-pad and sat on the divan, stretching his long legs before him. As he organized his thoughts, he rubbed the jewel hanging from his neck, thinking of his partner. His partner, lover, friend, mate. His. Tristan, who'd been absent since their wondrous night in the forest. The night he'd learned they were all but married.

Tristan. Where the fuck are you?

He laughed to himself, thinking he sure enjoyed the honeymoon without the benefit of a spouse. If his plans went the way he hoped…

Chapter Eighteen

Today was the day. The one ordained by the Divinity long before Phoenix Ashe had emerged from an innocuous incubation chamber. It had been foretold, a masc with the face of an angel and a complexion as mercurial as his moods would someday reunite the prefecture.

He'd spent several auroras talking with his prelate, going through the ancient recordings of the Divinity's chosen. Though their voices were garbled and at times indistinguishable, their message was clear as polymer. Phoenix Ashe was *the* one. He wore the Divinity's color—aquamarine. Tristan's eyes matched the stone around his neck. She had made her intent known. Tristan Faire and Phoenix Ashe were destined partners. They would work together to bring about the changes needed to fulfill the ancient prophecies.

Not only had Phoenix sought his cleric's counsel, he'd met with the current administration's city council. After many discussions, some of them heated, they had come up with a plan Phoenix intended to unveil at his swearing-in ceremony.

With the sun's resplendence in a cloudless sky, he would be sworn in as the youngest mayor of Prefecture Staquo. He was inexperienced, uncertain but prepared to the best of his ability.

"Are you ready, Phoenix?"

"Yes, sir." Phoenix stood next to Galen Ashe, thinking about the differences between his sole, eminent parent and Tristan's warm family. He wished for the physician's blessing, but chided himself for not having the courage to inform him of the contents of his inaugural speech. He feared Galen would suffer a heart infarction when he heard Phoenix's address.

His parent spared naught, expressing his doubts about Phoenix's appearance and pointing out it was barely satisfactory.

"Why do you insist on wearing that Divinity-awful, gaudy jewel?"

"It's a gift from a friend, and I like it."

"It's completely inappropriate for the occasion," Galen remarked with a huff. He walked away, shaking his head, and called for their ride.

When the luxury air-transport appeared on his private landing, Phoenix hoped his parent wouldn't pay heed to his skin's sudden pallor. His hands trembled, but if Galen noticed, he'd likely attribute their shaking to his son's nervousness over becoming mayor, rather than his fear of altitudes. With a deep, fortifying breath, Phoenix stepped into the conveyance for the long and scenic trip to City Hall.

They would circle the prefecture five times as the traditional rituals required. The flyover gave Phoenix the opportunity to take in the purlieus under his direction. He forced himself to look out over his city and view the crowds assembling for the inauguration. Femmes filled the streets as they walked from Hybridia into Segratia. Their colorful garb was unmistakable, and their proud stride made him wonder if Tristan Faire was among them.

People were coming to witness Phoenix take his oath from as far away as Portside. The turnout of his constituents humbled him unlike anything he'd ever known. He swore he spied Qandi Kane in the crowd. He was glad the old femme had joined the festivities, despite all the grumbling he'd done when Phoenix had invited him.

"Where are we headed?" Galen's disapproving voice interrupted Phoenix's musings. He looked up and realized the transport had turned toward the Outlying area.

"As tradition requires, we are surveying the prefecture."

"No one expects you to canvass the wilderness. There's nothing there worth your concern."

"I'm sorry, sir. But you are wrong. Beneath the canopy of trees live the Outlyers. Like it or not, they are my constituents and deserving of my consideration. After we greet them…the required five times…we will pay our respects to Canopia."

"Canopia? Really, Phoenix. That is completely unnecessary. They're rabble. Farmers and mixed breeds. You do yourself a disservice. What a waste of time and precious mintage."

"Doesn't matter. They are my people and I am to become their mayor. I *will* give them my due respect."

"Hmpf. Like I said, a total waste of your time."

"I can drop you off, if you like. Perhaps you could wait with the Arch Prelate for me to complete the ritual obeisance."

"Nonsensical tradition, if you ask me. They should pay you homage. Not the other way around."

"My revered parent, I respect your concerns and I understand you have been living under the misguidance that persecution of the Outlyers and Canopians is the Divinity's will. I assure you, it was not her decree. I plan to right a wrong that has been five-thousand spans in the making."

"Well said, Phoenix Ashe," Terra Gaia's lilting voice praised him, coaxing him to smile. *"You will make a fine mayor. I'll see you soon, my darling son."*

Phoenix gazed wistfully at the small village as they flew over and shook his head at Terra's endearment. He'd asked her not to refer to him as her son, but she would not be deterred, assuring him it was the proper form of address. Once again, he wondered if Tristan would come watch him take his oath.

"Are you paying attention?" Galen's gruff demeanor saddened Phoenix as he turned away from the window to attend his parent. As they approached Segratia, he redirected the transport to let the physician off on his private platform. Galen could call for another to take him the short distance to City Hall. Phoenix had a ritual to complete.

"I will see you at the reception, sir."

"Perhaps for a moment, then I must go. There are patients to examine. As always."

Phoenix shook his head, knowing he'd never change his parent. Galen Ashe was as the Divinity made him — a brilliant and handsome masc and a skilled physician. His demeanor he'd learned from his parent, who'd learned it from his, who'd learned it… Phoenix hoped his parent and his constituents were ready to assimilate something new.

With each passing of his transport over the prefecture, Phoenix noticed the crowds were swelling rather than diminishing. He realized Wiccan, Terra and Tristan's parents had been busy spreading the word of his proposed changes. From among the Outlying areas, there was rustling under the trees' massive canopy. They too were on the move into the city.

Upon completing his final pass over the domain, Phoenix arrived at City Hall. His advisors rushed him away from prying eyes once he'd alighted from the conveyance. They led him to a room within the building he would soon know as well as he knew his own pinnacle apartment. But, for now, he was completely turned around and at their mercy. When they ushered him into a windowless room not much larger than his closet, he gasped at seeing Terra, Wiccan, Riley and Loren waiting for him. He glanced around the small space, expecting to spot Tristan with his family.

"No, my darling. He's not here," Terra said.

"How can he stay away for so long? And, today of all days," Phoenix whined, hating the way he sounded. So needy and forlorn, not mayor-like in the least.

"Wiccan, Terra. Can you give us a few moments alone with Phoenix?" Loren said.

Terra looked like she was about to argue. She glanced from Phoenix to Riley and to Wiccan. She opened her mouth but before she could argue Loren stopped her.

"Please," Loren begged, leaving Phoenix to wonder what was so urgent. He couldn't pick up anything disturbing in their thoughts. But they were Tristan's parents and had spent his lifetime concealing their intentions from his telepathy when it suited them. With a tiny nod to him, Terra took Wiccan's hand and left the trio alone.

"Phoenix, love. Tristan's not coming back," Riley said, staring into his eyes and holding his hand as if the kind gesture would ease the sting of his words.

"What! Has he contacted you? Where has he gone?"

"He won't return until *you* reach out to him," Loren said.

"How can I, when no one will tell me where he has fucking gone off to?"

"It's not that we won't tell you. It's that we don't know. He hasn't contacted us."

"What about Terra? Surely she knows where he is. It's not like Terra to stay out of her son's thoughts for long," Phoenix said.

"We have asked her, and she tells us she refuses to get in the middle of a lover's spat. She won't seek out Tris unless he contacts her."

"Fine fucking time to give him privacy," Phoenix grumbled, annoyed at the woman whose inability to stay out of her son's head was fodder for mothering jokes. Phoenix adored her, but her damned ill-timed conscience pissed him off.

"*Swearing will not endear me to your cause, Phoenix Ashe.*" Terra's voice broke into his head.

"*Leave it to you to insist on being present even when asked to give us privacy. If you weren't so likable, I would banish you to the Outlying area. But knowing you, Terra Gaia, you would organize my reclusive constituents and overthrow my burgeoning administration.*"

"Damn right I would. Instead of grumbling, focus your energies on calling my son to your side. He's a remarkable telepath. Believe me. He will hear you."

"Terra's right," Riley said.

"I'm sorry, I didn't quite get that." Terra's lyrical laugh rang out beyond the door just as her thoughts resonated in their heads.

"I said you were right, Terra. Now quit eavesdropping and get back in here."

"Yes, stop your infernal meddling and help us. We have a mayor to ready."

Phoenix grinned and shouted when Terra and Wiccan returned, announcing they had brought him a surprise. Qandi Kane strode in behind them with feather boas, sparkling shoes and glittering rings all competing for attention.

"Qandi! It's good to see you again. Are the Dawsons with you?" Phoenix hugged the aging femme, careful not to squeeze too hard or crush his flamboyant garb.

"No, boy. You think we're attached at the nether regions? They have been too busy for an old femme, what with you assigning them research and all."

"Now, Qandi. You're not old, you're the Divinity's reflection. You should be proud. But why are you here? Not that I'm not happy to see you."

"Terra thought you might need my help. Said you were gorgeous, but you possess the fashion sense of an Outlyer."

Inwardly, Phoenix feared his friend would want him to wear a kaleidoscope of glitter-enhanced feathers. "I'm grateful for your help, my friend. What did you have in mind?"

"Don't go getting your twaddle in an uproar. All I brought was this here cape and my makeup case. You could use a little color in your cheeks and a bit of kohl around your eyes. Give those stuffy Elitists an inauguration the bards will write about for a thousand spans."

"Trust him, darling. Qandi will do right by you," Riley reassured him. "Because if he doesn't, he'd have to face Terra."

"Stop it. I am *not* all that bad," Terra said with a scowl as she ushered everyone but Qandi from the overfilled room. "Remember what I said, Phoenix. Concentrate your energy on calling him." With a reassuring glance and blowing him a kiss, she and the entourage left Phoenix alone with his stylist. He rocked on his heels and waited.

"Now, sit and quit fidgeting. You're wiggling more than my ass on docking day." Phoenix glanced at him in confusion. "You know, trying to attract the attention of sailors on shore leave."

"Oh. I get it," Phoenix said followed by a wry grin. "Sorry, my mind's occupied with Tristan and these tedious preparations. But, I'm all yours."

While Qandi regaled him with stories of past docking days, Phoenix took Terra's advice to heart and spent the time thinking hard about Tristan. He wished he'd return in time for the inaugural ceremony. While Qandi applied the proposed makeup, Phoenix recalled his and Tristan's times together. His inaugural deposit, their hot tub interlude, the night in the forest—he couldn't get them out of his mind.

"I don't know what's going on in your gorgeous head, but whatever it might be is ruining the makeup. Every time it's just right, your skin darkens and I must start over. Besides, if you don't do something about that tempting boner, you will ruin the line of your robe."

"I'm sorry, Qandi. I'll try to rein in my libido. I miss Tristan and want him here with me. I need his strength to get me through all this craziness. Can you imagine? I'm about to become the mayor. I'm afraid and if Tristan were here, he'd know what to say to calm me."

"He hasn't left you, Phoenix Ashe. How do you not realize this? He is with you here, in your heart and here, in your head." Qandi put a hand over Phoenix's chest and pressed a chaste kiss against his temple. "And if you look deep enough, you'll recognize he is residing within your soul."

"I hope you're right."

"Count on it. Now, let me finish."

"Okay, but not too much."

"I'll change the hue of the blusher so it highlights your gorgeous cheekbones no matter how your skin tone changes. A hint of kohl on your eyelids, to make the femmes pee themselves, and a hint of — "

Phoenix's boisterous laughter rang out, scaring Qandi, who grabbed his chest as if he were having an infarction. "Oh, Qandi. You are delightful. I thank the Divinity for leading me to the Portside Tavern. Without her intervention, I wouldn't have met you."

"I assure you, your eminence, the pleasure is mine. Now let this old femme finish his job."

Phoenix sat still and remained quiet while Qandi fussed. He let his thoughts turn to Tristan, but kept a careful rein on his musings. He had no desire to stray into the more lascivious moments of their relationship moments before taking the stage. He sighed as Qandi brushed his hair until it shone, recalling how much Tristan loved the tresses and how he wrapped his fingers in his strands. Focusing on those tender moments, especially the ones following transcendence, gave him a measure of much-needed calm.

"All done. Stand up and you can put on the robe."

Phoenix rose and stared at himself in the full-length mirror hidden away in a cupboard. He didn't recognize himself with his cheeks blushed and his eyes lined. His hair shone like the gossamer wings of the Divinity's seraphim.

"I take it back," Qandi said holding his palm against his cheek and gazing at Phoenix.

"You take what back?"

"It won't be just the femmes soiling themselves. Mascs and hybrids and likely the hetero women will all join in. I'm afraid your ceremony is doomed to become a virtual pee-fest."

"Better that, than crying tears of regret and flooding the streets."

"You don't give yourself enough credit, Phoenix Ashe. The populace looks forward to your government. Word of the changes you're planning has circulated through the purlieus. How else do you count for the size of the crowd awaiting your appearance?"

"They have nothing else to do and I'm the only game in town?"

"Now you jest. Keep your sense of humor and do right by your constituents. The rest is window dressing. I hear the music has stopped. That means the old prelate will make your introduction soon. Let's get you robed."

When Qandi finished fussing, Phoenix was garbed neck to toe in a black silk robe. Beneath its luxurious folds he wore pristine white pantaloons and a shirt of the finest Portside fabric. The linen had been transported from a neighboring prefecture beyond the

Paradrae Sea for the occasion. The near-transparent material hugged Phoenix's body, contouring to every muscle and highlighting his considerable endowments. Tristan's pendant lay in the hollow of his neck. Over the garments, his friend had placed the simple robe. Qandi opened the dressing room door and bowed his head in deference to the mayor-to-be.

As a show of his humility, Phoenix strode the distance to the inaugural stage and up its stairs in his bare feet. His nerves hummed near the surface as he stood behind the partition separating him and the audience. He waited for the Arch Prelate to introduce him. *Breathe, Phoenix. Just breathe.*

"...we humbly ask for the Divinity's blessing." The prelate's prayer for the prefecture ended, signaling Phoenix's introduction was next. His ears rang and his palms tingled. Sweat gathered on his skin, despite the diaphanous fabric he wore. His heart pounded, and he was certain all Segratia heard its erratic beat.

"May I present to you, a fine masc known to all, one of Segratia's esteemed sons, and the Divinity's chosen — our next mayor, Phoenix Ashe!"

Phoenix walked out from behind the concealing partition, bowed before the Arch Prelate and walked to the end of the stage. From his vantage point he looked out onto the assembled masses, searching for Tristan, but seeing only strangers. He bowed his head in deference to his constituency and waited for the applause to wane.

When it was silent, he stood next to his friend, who clapped him on the shoulder.

"Phoenix Ashe, it is my supreme honor to serve the Divinity's will and name you the next mayor of

Prefecture Staquo. Are you prepared to accept her decree?"

"I am, your Grace."

"Please, take a knee."

Phoenix kneeled in front of his prelate and bowed his head. His hair fell forward and hid his face from view. Phoenix knew the old cleric loved the drama of an inauguration and took his time, to allow the crowds to absorb his presence. Phoenix peeked at the large screen behind Thom and watched as he held up a gold circlet encrusted with the Divinity's stones — triangular cut aquamarines. Phoenix stared as mesmerized as the crowd, watching the Arch Prelate lift the coronet high overhead, until the sun's rays caught the jewels and reflected their brilliance back to the assembly. Phoenix loved his prelate and he knew Thom loved him as if he had contributed to his emergence. With Galen Ashe away so much, the cleric had helped to raise him. Phoenix had often spent more time with the prelate than his esteemed parent. His love for the Thom Didymas overflowed.

The Arch Prelate placed the ring of gems upon his head. It's substantial weight surprising him. "Rise, Phoenix Ashe, and face your people, here from all corners of Prefecture Staquo. They have come to witness our rituals and your ascension into the office of mayor." Phoenix stood and faced the eclectic assembly. "I ask you, are you prepared to take charge of your responsibilities with honor, respect and love for your citizens?"

"I am, your Grace." Phoenix's voice rang out, his confident response loud and clear. From his vantage he saw much of the crowd watching the ceremony on the holo-screens which had been installed on each side of the stage and amid the park into which the crowd overflowed. He was glad to see no one would miss the proceeding if they wanted to see it.

"Will you listen with an open mind to the advice of your council? Will you seek your prelate's counsel when your heart is troubled?"

"I will, your Grace."

"Do you swear on the tenets of our faith to put the needs of your people first above all else?"

"I do, your Grace."

"You have made the five circumnavigations of the prefecture. Each bypass represents your promise to those who call themselves mascs, femmes, heteros, sapphics and hybrids that we are one people in the eyes of the Divinity. We are one people in your heart. Is this the truth as you know it?"

"Yes, your Grace."

"Is this the truth you will defend?"

"Most humbly, your Grace."

"You may rise and face your constituency. People of Prefecture Staquo. I give you your new leader, Mayor Phoenix Ashe."

Thunderous applause filled the air. Shouts of 'Phoenix, Phoenix, Phoenix' were heard all around. He scanned the crowd, seeking the faces that were the dearest to him. He spotted Loren and Riley, and Wiccan Tall, who towered above them. They smiled and waved. He wondered where Terra had gonedisappeared to, but she couldn't have gone too far. From the size of the crowd, moving was near impossible.

Phoenix listened to the comments that came his way from the crowd, proclaiming he made a splendid sight standing tall and proud. He appreciated their awe at the contrast of his white hair against the richness of his black robe. He caught a glimpse of himself on the holoscreens, mesmerized by the green-blue hue of his crown's stones casting an aura of power around his form. His kohl-lined eyes burned with pride to serve his people. Phoenix waved and smiled until his cheeks hurt.

He was about to step behind the podium and make his inaugural speech when he felt a peculiar warmth around his throat and head. He squashed his first reaction, to cast off the jewelry, and let the heat seep into him, because how could anything that held the Divinity's stones or something Tristan had given him cause him harm? He embraced the sensations and opened his robe, holding his arms wide and revealing the robe's shining aquamarine lining. Tristan's pendant glowed at his throat.

Chapter Nineteen

Phoenix touched the jewel, unintentionally drawing attention to it. A rolling murmur built throughout the throng of onlookers. He ignored it in favor of stepping behind the podium to make his speech. He couldn't ignore the intensifying heat around his neck and scanned the crowd once more for Terra. Perhaps she might have some insight about the jewel's transformation. He thought he saw her talking to someone, but couldn't catch her eye. He was too unnerved to try shouting and drawing her attention.

He waited for the crowd to quiet before he began speaking.

"Good afternoon. I am humbled you have taken time out to attend my little induction as your mayor. I promise to you and the Divinity I will serve you to the best of my capabilities. I also wish to thank my friend, Arch Prelate Thom Didymas, for administering the mayoral oaths.

"Now, time to get down to business. I understand there has been talk of the changes I plan to make. My good friend Qandi Kane, yes, I can see by your expressions many of you know him."

There were good natured chuckles all around and Qandi himself swinging one of his boas overhead.

"Anyway, Qandi tells me that you all are eager to hear what the plans are for our prefecture. First, I want to say that prejudice and discrimination have been prevalent in our lives far too long. As of today, it will no longer be tolerated. Respect and equality is the law of the land and the will of the Divinity. My brethren and sistren, with this in mind, I am making the following changes, each designed to facilitate the survival and well-being of all our citizens.

"After lengthy discussions with the council and input from my own esteemed parent, we are investing in new incubation chambers. I am also tripling the number with half of the new machines to be exclusive for the next five spans to the femme population at no cost." A collective gasp and surprised murmurs rolled through the crowd. Phoenix waited a moment before continuing. "I'm not certain if you are all aware, but their numbers are perilously close to endangered. It is our hope that the easy access to the chambers will stop their march to extinction. In addition, education in the Hybridia purlieu has been woefully neglected. Until the local school is suitable for use, the children will be welcomed into the masc education system, from here on out known as the Prefecture Staquo Schools.

"I've had the pleasure of visiting the Outlying area and meeting with many of its citizens. For eons, we Segratians have taken their bounty with little regard for their needs. I have met with Canopians, mostly farmers and artisans and their children. I have shared sustenance at their tables. The prefecture has done itself a huge disservice by not allowing heteros to own property. They are clever people, and we can learn from their ingenuity.

"To that end, I'd like to introduce to you Wiccan Tall and Terra Gaia. They have graciously agreed to chair the new Artisans Committee. For the time being they will be housed in the mayoral mansion, which once renovated will also house the new Agricultural Committee. Loren and Riley Faire have promised to lend their expertise until it is time to harvest their next crops. The land which was appropriated by our previous administrator to grow covfefe, we will lease to those city dwellers who wish to contribute to the sustenance of our population.

"To the Outlyers, I offer you this. Free transportation to the prefecture schools until such time as your new school buildings are completed, and we have hired competent staff to oversee your children's education. The way the villages have been ignored is an abomination, not only to myself but to the Divinity as well. Beginning today, I intend to right this wrong.

"To the sapphics, I promise you are to be welcomed into the city and surrounding purlieus. Segratia, Hybridia and Portside have suffered sorely without your influence. Please accept my apologies and my invitation to meet with me on the morrow to discuss your particular needs and form a committee to help with the transitions. I say it is time for you and the hybrids to emerge from the shadows of our society and take part in the making of your futures.

"My fellow mascs. I can hear your grumblings from here, but I also sense your insecurities. You're wondering how these changes will affect your life. Will you lose your Elitist status? Will you forfeit your fine apartment? Your stature? Your access to incubation chambers? Believe me, I understand your misgivings. However, I am counting on you to lead and to learn. The purlieus have need of your expertise. I challenge you to mentor your neighbors as they learn the ways of business, as they trust their children into our care, and as they venture into a society previously denied to them. We are Segratians, and we are the Divinity's children. Our actions reflect her love.

"One of the challenges I'd like the mascs to consider is the depositories. I realize we have utilized the facilities not only to save our inaugural deposit, but as pleasure houses, relegating the attendants to little more than high-paid courtesans. There must be a more productive use of the facilities and its people. Also on the morrow, I will meet with the depository directors and several masc businessmen to come up with a plan to integrate the facilities into the new societal restructure.

"While researching the ancient recordings with the Arch Prelate, and talking with Terra Gaia, a remarkable, if on occasions intrusive, telepath, I learned all the prefecture's citizens were born with psychic abilities. However, much of the populace have let them wane until they are rudimentary at best. The femmes have nurtured and expanded their capabilities. I'd like to encourage everyone to attend the Center of Telepathic Expansion. Once again, Terra Gaia has guided me in this endeavor. Once we have nailed down the details, holo-messages will be delivered to each household with options.

"This restructure is a huge undertaking and will not be successful without your support. The numerous constructions and remodels will open countless job opportunities to skilled workers and mentorships for those wanting to learn a new skill.

"The last thing I want to address is the disservice that has been done to many of our population. For five thousand spans the laws have stated mascs must mate with mascs. Femmes are meant for femmes.

"Mixed couples, hybrids, those attracted to mascs and femmes, and sapphic singular women. These fruitful members of our society have been denied the sanctity of marriage. No more. From this day on, it is the law of Prefecture Staquo to honor marriages, sanctified by the Divinity and legalized by the government to all couples regardless of singularity or duality."

Phoenix watched the faces he could see and noted their surprise. There were a few disgusted expressions on mascs and femmes. For the most part, he saw joy. Mixed couples kissed openly, reveling in their government's newfound acceptance. Phoenix grinned and turned to the Arch Prelate. "You're going to be very busy in the coming weeks with all the weddings you'll perform, your grace."

"Not a burden. Not a burden at all. I rather look forward to the novelty of a mixed wedding."

"As do I," Phoenix said with a wink, thinking of Tristan.

"I'm not certain what you're contemplating, but your complexion darkens and your pendant glows even brighter, the more we speak of mixed couples."

Phoenix thanked Thom once more for his part in his inauguration. He fingered the pendant which continued to grow warmer the more he thought of Tristan.

Ah, love. Where are you? I need you.

Silence. Phoenix doubted he'd ever possessed psychic powers to begin with. Perhaps they only worked with Tristan and his family. Maybe the Canopians acted like conductors, enhancing his meager abilities. With a few final words of encouragement and thanks to his constituents, Phoenix raised his arms high in the air, praising the Divinity for the prefecture's good fortunes. He bowed five times, acknowledging each contingent. Then, he went behind the partition to gather his thoughts and to change clothes before making an appearance at the reception.

"I have but one question. Where do you intend living if you've given away the mansion to my mother?"

"Tristan!" Phoenix's feet felt glued to the floor as he took in his lover's surprise appearance. Gone were the rainbow-hued braids. He had colored his hair yellow, and he'd chosen to wear it loose. His pantaloons and shirt hung from his narrow frame like wet noodles. He'd lost weight, his cheeks hollow and his hands appearing skeletal.

Did I do that to him? Broken his heart to the point of emaciation? Divinity, forgive me.

"She does, my love, and so do I. Now come here and kiss me."

If he could have, Phoenix would have launched himself at Tristan and tumbled with him onto the floor. But since he was a dignified masc who was six and one half cubits, heavier than his mate, and the newly initiated mayor, he took two steps to stand in front of the femme. His femme. He stretched out his hand to caress the face he'd missed more than he believed possible, whimpering when Tristan leaned in to his touch.

Phoenix picked him up and tossed him over his shoulders like a sack of Canopian grain, ignoring his half-hearted protests. He didn't put him down until they were behind the dressing room door and he had locked it. He had questions, and he wanted answers. But first he *needed* kisses.

He kissed Tristan until they couldn't breathe. Then, he did it again. Tongue, teeth, lips, he couldn't get enough of his lover, his friend, his destined mate. He ran his hands over Tristan's chest, shocked at the amount of muscle he had lost. It didn't matter — thin or strong, he loved him above all else. He needed to show him and he had to do it *now*.

Phoenix Ashe, the Mayor of Prefecture Staquo, went to his knees. He opened the codpiece on Tristan's pants, though he could have easily pulled them down his slim hips. Tristan's thick cock sprang from a nest of yellow curls, surprising Phoenix. He was accustomed to seeing his sac denuded. He buried his face in the wiry hairs and inhaled his familiar scent.

Divinity, I'm addicted to his smell.

Phoenix clasped Tristan's ass as his femme leaned against the door. He kneaded the muscles and wondered if his lover knew how much he wanted him, how much he had missed him.

"I know. I've missed you, too. Please, my love, suck me."

Phoenix kissed the tip of Tristan's cock before taking his thick length into his mouth. He savored his lover's flavor and drank his copious pre-seminal fluids. He ran his tongue along the thick vein and thought he'd never tire of this feast. Thirty spans ago, he'd emerged from an incubation chamber for this purpose — to love this gorgeous femme who completed him.

Tristan wrapped his hands in Phoenix's hair, tugging at his scalp as he fought the urge to fuck the mayor's mouth. He had waited an eternity for Phoenix to realize the truth of the divine prophecies. But he didn't want to ponder the spirituality of their joining. Not now. He concentrated on the carnality and the pleasure coursing through him from Phoenix's talented mouth. Wet heat engulfed his cock as he slid it deeper into Phoenix's throat. His lover was good at this, taking his length without gagging, letting him savor his muscles as they swallowed around his sensitive flesh. Unable to stop himself, he tightened his grip on Phoenix's hair and fucked his mouth with abandon.

"Yes. Yes. A million times yes. I love your mouth. So incredible." He was near to incoherent with pleasure and couldn't help but babble.

Within his mind Tristan heard Phoenix's voice, telling him he tasted like fine Segratian wine, how much he wanted him and what he'd do to him once he'd finished fattening him back up. Tristan stifled a giggle because it was never good to laugh while his dick was vulnerable between a set of sharp teeth. Instead he listened to his lover, reveling in the knowledge Phoenix had established their psychic joining on his own! This feat had never happened outside the depository. Not with a masc. His lover's psychic abilities amazed and excited him.

He'd heard Phoenix calling out for him to return home. Not responding to the constant tugging on his conscience had nearly undone him. He couldn't name one solid reason why he'd waited until today to answer his pleas. There would be time to dissect their relationship and mistakes later. For now, the love of his life — the mayor — was on his knees and sucking his cock like he couldn't get enough. *Enjoy it, Tristan!*

Tristan leaned his head back against the door and savored the sensations coursing through him. Lightening-like heat coalesced in his sac and shot up his spine as every muscle tensed to the point of pain. He stood on trembling legs, poised on the brink of orgasm, begging to plummet over its edge into the oblivion of climactic bliss.

"I've got you. Let me drink your essence. I love you. Mind. Body. Soul. For eternity." Phoenix's voice growled in Tristan's consciousness, sending him tumbling into the sweetest orgasm he'd known. Jets of hot cum filled Phoenix's mouth as Tristan shouted his ecstasy to the rafters. With a final spurt of his seminal fluid, he cried out his love for Phoenix Ashe, unmindful who might have been listening to their passion on the other side of the walls. Then he collapsed onto the floor, trusting Phoenix would keep from harm.

Realizing Tristan could no longer hold himself upright, Phoenix sat back on his haunches and cradled him in his arms, murmuring honeyed words into his ear. Tristan petted his cheek and commented on his darkened complexion.

"I'm sorry to leave you in such an unsatisfied state, love. I fear at the moment I don't have the energy to meet your needs."

"It doesn't matter, as long as I met yours. The rest can wait. There's a lifetime ahead of us. You come first, my love. Allow me to take care of you."

Tristan smiled and gazed into Phoenix's eyes and nodded. The soft smile soon faded as he closed his eyes and slept. He was oblivious when Qandi Kane opened the mysteriously unlocked door and walked in.

"I've taken the liberty of calling a transport for you, your eminence," he whispered, eyeing the sleeping form in Phoenix's embrace.

"Thank you, Qandi. I appreciate your thoughtfulness, but how did you get in?"

"The Divinity."

"Hmm. I'm not going to argue, though I think Terra Gaia may have located a key and slipped it to you. That would account for her absence during my speech. Will you make my apologies at the reception? I fear I may not make an appearance until late tonight. Tristan needs rest and sustenance."

"I will, your—"

"Please, no formalities. I'm still Phoenix and wish my friends to address me as such."

"But—"

"Please, Qandi."

"Of course, your eminence."

Phoenix rose, careful with the precious cargo in his arms, and chuckled at Qandi's stubbornness. "Later, my friend. Thank you for all you have done on my behalf."

"A little makeup, some fabric. It wasn't much. Not compared to what you've put in motion for the prefecture. You go on home and rest with your partner. We will all meet you at the reception later."

Phoenix nodded, then strode from the room to meet his awaiting air-transport. He groaned at the flying conveyance but acknowledged it was a better choice because of the crowded thoroughfares. Without waking Tristan, he settled them into the seats and proceeded home.

The transport landed on the empty street in front of Tristan's cottage. Phoenix wondered if Terra had also arranged for the door to be left unsecured when it opened unexpectedly. He startled Loren and Riley as they were leaving the premises.

"Sorry, love. We didn't think you'd be back quite so soon. Terra said —"

"Never mind what she said. What's wrong with our son? Why isn't he awakening?"

"He's exhausted and from what I can tell he hasn't been eating well."

"That's an understatement. The boy looks positively emaciated," Galen Ashe said as he approached from a conveyance which had landed behind Phoenix's.

"Sir, what are you doing here?"

"Come, Phoenix. Put the boy in his bed and let me have a look at him." Phoenix hastened to do his parent's bidding, completely taken by surprise at his appearance. "His mother was quite concerned when she pulled me away from your reception. Which, by the way, you are quite tardy."

"I'm sorry. But Tristan comes first."

"So I've been told. Quite colorfully in fact. Terra Gaia has a rather...flamboyant mastery of the Gemin language."

"That's our girl," Loren said, winking at Riley, who burst out laughing. Despite his concern about Tristan, Phoenix laughed too. He also had been a recipient of her formidable flamboyancy.

Everyone followed Phoenix, who laid Tristan on his bed. The femme groaned, but didn't open his eyes.

"Out now. All of you. Let me examine my patient."

With a backward glance at his parent, Phoenix went with Loren and Riley into the living quarters to wait.

He paused to turn on the holo-screen, because the sights and sounds of the Paradrae Sea always comforted him.

"How did you know to come here?" Phoenix asked the couple sitting on the divan while he paced.

"Terra asked us to bring over some of your things. Said you'd be moving in with Tris once you 'got your head out of your posterior.'" Phoenix's eyebrows shot upward in astonishment.

"Like your parent said. She's flamboyant," Riley said with a giggle.

"Anyway, we put a portmanteau for you in Tris' room. I hope we brought over enough to get you through the next few days."

"I appreciate your consideration. Thank you," Phoenix said, pacing back and forth certain he was wearing a hole in the floor covering. Not even the sounds of the Paradrae Sea could calm him. *What's taking so long?*

Galen Ashe finally came out of Tristan's room wearing a frown. He glanced at the three worried faces watching him.

"He's sleeping. He requires sustenance and libations. Here are some additives. Put these in his food for the next dozen meals. You should also add these to his liquids for the next fourteen auroras."

"Thank you, Dr. Ashe. But what's wrong with him?" Loren asked.

"From what I gathered the short time he was awake, is that he has spent too much time consuming fermented libations and very little sustenance. He also lived off blue-grain bread. While the fare is good for stemming the hangover, it holds little nutritional value, unless there are additives in the loaves."

"Is there more we can do to help?" Riley asked, grasping his husband's hand.

"Phoenix, he needs rest and time to put back on the weight he's lost. It will take a while until he's gotten his energy and stamina back. Refrain from the sexual escapades until I've ascertained his health is back to normal."

"Yes, sir," Phoenix said, hoping his parent didn't know about his recent reunion activity with Tristan.

"I'm certain his parents can back me up here. Femme's expend more energy than we Mascs. It has something to do with them using their psychic abilities as well as their physical attributes. The results are incredible, but often costly to them."

"It's how we stay so trim," Loren said.

"Genetically, there's no difference between mascs and femmes. Our muscle mass comes from the hours spent in the solar powered muscle stimulating chambers."

"I hated having to frequent the myo-chambers. It was uncomfortable and boring," Phoenix said.

"Yes. But look at you now. You are the ultimate Masc with musculoskeletal perfection. You were destined to become Mayor and your time in the chambers prepared you for the job. Do you not recall the holo-recordings you absorbed while you were developing your physique?"

"I do. So, you're saying the Femmes remain lithe because they expend more energy than we do."

"Partly, but also because their diets are better. Loren and Riley can attest the farm fare contributes to their sleek builds."

"He's right. There's more tempting sustenance in the city. Besides the physical labor on the farm, keeps us in shape."

"At any rate, mind my orders and take care of Tristan Faire. I will see you later this eventide." At Phoenix's dumfounded expression, Galen added, "Your reception? Your presence is expected. Good day gentlemen."

Phoenix walked with his parent to the door, and put his arms around him, ignoring his attempt to shrug off the unfamiliar contact. "Thank you...Father. I love Tristan and I can't express my gratitude at your solicitousness."

"You're welcome, son."

"I love you too, you know," Phoenix shouted as his father stepped into his conveyance. Galen turned, disbelief on his wrinkled face. Then a smile broke out and it was as if the sun had burst from behind a cloud to warm Phoenix's heart.

Chapter Twenty

While Phoenix waited for Tristan to awaken, he, Loren and Riley busied themselves in the food prep area, making enough meals for the next three auroras. Phoenix let the two femmes manage the dishes while he created nutritious libations. He had to use his holo-pad to connect with his robo-servant and extract the recipes. He could have called for a technician to program Tristan's servant, but he wanted to take care of his partner himself. Besides keeping busy, kept his mind off his part in Tristan's condition.

"Don't blame yourself, my darling," Riley said, picking up on Phoenix's thoughts. "It's not your fault he didn't eat. Nor is it your failing that Tris refused sustenance and lived on fermented libations."

"If anything, the responsibility is ours. As his parents, we should have tried harder to locate him," Loren said, stirring the nutrient additive into the dish he was creating.

"I know you believe that, my love. But Tris is full-grown. He *chose* to do this to himself."

"But—"

"It was a *bad* choice, but still, letting himself deteriorate to the point of emaciation was his doing. We will intervene and do what we can until good health is his again. But I won't let him draw us into a cycle of inebriation and sobering like so many of those poor souls in Portside."

"You won't have to worry about him that way. I swear, Loren and Riley, I love your son and I promise not to do anything again to drive him away. Together we will make you proud," Phoenix said, still holding on to his guilt. He was the one who'd dismissed Tristan's feelings until he felt he had to leave. Phoenix vowed not to repeat the same mistake. He stirred the libation he was mixing then poured it into a container for refrigeration. There was enough left to fill a glass for Tristan and one for himself. He'd need the extra fortification to get through the night, when all he wanted was to crawl into bed with Tristan and hold him.

"Phoenix," Tristan called from the bedroom. Riley jumped to help his son, but Loren restrained him, reminding his partner Tris had asked for Phoenix.

"If he needs us, I'm positive the mayor will tell us."

"You're right. I'm sorry, Phoenix. Go to him," Riley conceded with a nod. "Give him our love." Then he turned back to the sustenance he was preparing.

Phoenix picked up the drinks and thanked them. He walked into the bedroom to find Tristan sitting upright. He wanted to get out of bed, but Phoenix said no, and after setting the glasses down, fluffed the pillows and set them behind Tristan's head and back until he was comfortable.

"You need to rest," Phoenix said, brushing the hair from his lover's eyes. His heart broke at his gaunt appearance and troubled gaze.

"There's nothing wrong with me that kissing you and loving on you won't fix."

"That's not quite true. But the fact is, we've been ordered to celibacy for the time being."

"Who said?" Tristan whined, looking and sounding like a mutinous child.

"Your esteemed physician...my father."

"I demand a second opinion." Tristan pouted.

"Fine, let me call Terra Gaia. I believe it was she who asked my parent to attend you."

"You don't play fair. Mother already expressed her opinions on my actions and appearance. I'll stay in bed...for the time being."

"Good. Now drink this. Doctor's decree."

"Tastes like oryx piss and grass."

"Must be the additives," Phoenix said after sipping from his glass and setting it aside with a grimace. "You're under orders to add them to your libations for the next fourteen auroras. Penance for holing up in Portside with nothing but gin and blue-grain bread."

"I'm sorry, Phoenix. I didn't plan to stay away so long, and I didn't intend to drink myself into this state. I must look divinity-awful."

"You're still the most beautiful thing I've seen since I left you in Canopia."

"Hmpf. You don't get out much, do you?"

"Funny guy. I'm serious, but I am surprised the Dawsons and Qandi Kane allowed you to wallow."

"They didn't know I was there. I stayed away from the more reputable establishments and the possibility of meeting someone who knows me. Instead, I chanced upon Dorian Seaborn. I hadn't seen him since Seminal Depository fired him. He was angry and blamed me for his downfall. He spent a lot of time grumbling that the only place he could find work was in the Portside whore houses."

"I hope you don't expect me to feel bad for him, because when I hear his name my ass clenches and my cock burns from the memory of his tender ministrations," Phoenix said, his voice dripping with sarcasm.

"I understand your animosity and you have every right to your feelings, but Dorian and I were friends for many spans. I was furious with him, but as time went by, I grew less angry. Not that I forgive him for hurting you."

"Why are we talking about Dorian Seaborn?"

"I don't know. I guess I wanted you to be aware I had fermented libations with him and—"

"Did you fuck him?"

"No! I swear on the Divinity scrolls. I would never cheat on you, Phoenix. I *love* you. We've transcended…more than once. That means something. I know you don't believe me and you prefer not to be partnered with me for the rest of your life, but I promise you there will be no one for me but you."

"I do believe you, and while we've been apart I've reconsidered and altered my thinking. But, we'll discuss this later, once you've regained your strength. Now, tell me why you stayed away so long. Didn't you hear me calling for you?"

"I heard you and listened to your doubts about us. I understood your belief you needed a masc for your life mate and I hated the thought. *I* was your life mate. The fermented libations made it so I couldn't hear you or feel your presence anymore. Yet, when I awakened your uncertainty filled my thoughts, and it became easier and less painful to spend my days incoherent. I let Dorian ply me with spirits and I fooled myself into believing he was still my friend."

"Why did you come back today?"

"Like I said. I regarded Dorian as a friend. Then three nights ago, he tried selling me to a couple of sailors who wanted a go at the infamous Tristan Faire from the display parades."

"What the fuck! I swear my first act as mayor will be to hunt the fool down and string him up by his genitalia. How dare he?"

"Phoenix, Staquo is an evolved society. We don't string people up any more."

"Damn it!"

"Calm yourself and let me finish my tale before Loren and Riley bust in demanding to know why we're taking so long to join them."

"Okay, I'm sorry. It's just the thought of anyone harming you or intending to hurt you in any manner brings out all my protective instincts. The feeling is completely foreign to me, but I wouldn't have it any other way."

"That is so sweet, and if I were up for it, I'd show you how happy you make me."

"Up for it or not, you make me happy too. Go on. Finish your story."

"The sailors, they weren't thrilled when I refused to service them. Before they could retaliate, I ran as fast as my drunken feet allowed, which wasn't all that quick. It was fortuitous they hadn't yet gained their land legs after months at sea. They didn't try all that hard to chase me. However, I happened upon an apothecary who mixed up a concoction he promised would purge the fermentation from my blood. I awoke in Hybridia this morning with no memory of how I got there. I had lost two days and nights because of my stupidity."

"Divinity, Tristan. Anything could have befallen you. Are you certain you're not hurt, haven't been assaulted or worse?"

"I'm fine, or I will be," Tristan said, brushing away Phoenix's concern. Truth was, he couldn't have denied whether he had been violated. He'd shared his uncertainty with Galen Ashe earlier, not realizing he was Phoenix's parent. The physician had given him a thorough examination and pronounced him undamaged. He'd also administered medication which would cleanse his system of any opportunistic infections…just in case. Tristan shook his head and rubbed his temples, trying in vain to purge the unwanted thoughts from his consciousness. Instead, he concentrated on completing his story and hearing Phoenix's intentions. Tristan peered into his lover's sable eyes, which were dark with worry, and said, "When I saw the crowds making their way to Segratia, I joined them. I listened to their musings and realized today was your inauguration. I'm sorry I wasn't here for you. I swear I meant to be. It was never my plan to miss it. Forgive me?"

"Of course you're forgiven, but only if you accept my apology for driving you away, for not having faith in your love…no, in *our* love. Truth was, I was afraid — more like terrified — of breaking convention and admitting I loved a femme. And not just any femme, but a premier attendant of Hybridia."

"I'm sorry. I can't change my past and I wouldn't want to."

"No, you misunderstand. I'm not ashamed of your vocation. I'm insecure. You have experiences I could never hope to attain and what if…"

Phoenix hesitated to continue, fearing Tristan would find him foolish and too needy to bother with. Then he felt his presence in his thoughts and realized Tristan already knew all his insecurities and he wanted him anyway. Loved him despite his faults.

"Phoenix, it's true. I have had innumerable sexual encounters and many of them were fantastic, but even more were mundane. I had a job, and I did it. But you are everything. You are the one — the only one — with whom I've transcended. I admit I behaved badly when you didn't embrace the experience, but that hasn't lessened my feelings for you. In my soul, I'm committed to you forever."

"Phoenix. Tristan. You will miss your reception if you don't get a move on." Loren's voice stopped Phoenix from replying.

"We're leaving now. We'll see you soon, my darlings. Remember what Galen said. No sex. Our boy needs his rest."

Phoenix rolled his eyes and Tristan blushed. "I know! I'll help Tristan dress and we'll be there in an hour." He glanced at Tristan, whose puzzled expression made Phoenix realize he didn't know about the reception Phoenix was committed to attend. "I have to go shake hands and thank everyone for their support. I'd like you to join me, but if you're not up to going out, you should stay home. I'll return as soon as I can escape."

"No. I've already botched the swearing-in ceremony. I won't miss this engagement. Besides, Terra told me there will be dancing and I intend to have at least one dance with the new mayor."

"Hmm. Then we better get all gussied up and leave. Let me help you bathe and dress."

"I'm not that weak. The libation may have tasted like piss, but it has already started working. Besides, if you wash me we'll never leave here. 'No sex' rule be damned."

"Go ahead, but I'm right here if you need me."

An hour later their air-transport landed on the private landing strip outside Phoenix's pinnacle apartment.

"What are we doing here? I thought we were appearing at your reception."

"We are. Since I gave the mansion to Terra and moved into your cottage—"

"You have?"

"Yes. Riley and Loren transferred my things in earlier. Like you said, I've given the mayoral residence up for your mother's committee, and the grounds to Wiccan's agricultural group. I must live somewhere. My apartment will serve as the official quarters for the eminent mayor of Prefecture Staquo, but Phoenix Ashe is living with his life mate in a small cottage with the most amazing aviary. Besides, the leasing manager was most accommodating. The entire floor below mine is now available for any formal occasions my position requires. Shall we?" Phoenix held out his arm to steady Tristan as they joined the partygoers.

"It's about time, my darlings," Terra greeted them with Wiccan standing at her side. Gone was the garb suitable for farming. They both looked fashionable in their dressy wear. Terra's long hair was swept up in the latest chic style, and Phoenix swore Qandi Kane had helped with her makeup. She was gorgeous and Wiccan, well, if Phoenix wasn't taken and Wiccan wasn't hetero…

"Come, my loves. Riley and Loren are beside themselves with worry." Phoenix watched as she led Tristan to greet his parents. A familiar voice stopped him.

"Phoenix, old friend. How are they hanging?" Temple asked. Phoenix gasped, wondering at Temple's audacity to be altogether unmindful that he was attending his formal reception for the newly sworn mayor. He seemed to have forgotten Phoenix Ashe was now *the* mayor. Phoenix curled his lip, ignoring the inappropriate remark, and glanced at Gareth Knightly, who stood next to him, holding a fermented libation and appearing as if he'd overindulged in Phoenix's hospitality. Gareth squinted his reddened eyes and shook his head.

"What gives, Phoenix?" His hostility was palatable as he extended an arm toward Tristan, splashing Temple with whatever his glass held.

"Mind yourself, Gareth," Phoenix cautioned.

"Never thought you'd come to your own shindig hanging on to that little whore." A red haze engulfed Phoenix's vision and before he could change his mind, he pulled back his arm, balled his hand and punched his former friend in the nose. Satisfaction blossomed in his chest at the crunch of bone beneath his fist.

"Wiccan!" he shouted, ignoring his guests and the questions swirling around him. The giant man pushed his way through the crowd to reach Phoenix's side. He glanced from the bleeding masc on the floor to Phoenix and back again. "Wiccan, will you please escort these two from the building and into a transport? I fear they have overstayed their welcome."

"Sure thing, your eminence. Gentlemen." Phoenix raised an eyebrow at the formal tone and address of his friend. The man pulled Gareth upright by the collar and latched on to Temple's arm with his other hand, pushing them none too gently from the ballroom. The revelers gave Phoenix another questioning look, hoping for an explanation. When their mayor continued ignoring them, they went on about their business. The curious onlookers parted as Phoenix made his way to Tristan's side.

"Are you all right?" Tristan asked.

"I'm fine. Just needed a little help to remove the rubbish. Wiccan will return shortly."

"Well done, Phoenix Ashe," Terra said.

"Did I miss something?" Tristan wanted to know, feeling like everyone was talking around him. *Have I become invisible?*

"No, my darling. Never," Terra, forever poking about in her son's thoughts, reassured him. "There's your secondary-father now. Wiccan," she called out. It wasn't like he couldn't locate her in a crowd. She was tiny, but she made a big impression.

"There you are," Qandi Kane greeted their small gathering. Behind him, swatting away boa feathers, were Elton and Bernie Dawson.

Elton congratulated Phoenix and Bernie seemed awestruck, talking with the mayor even though she'd served him libations in their Portside tavern.

"My friends. I'm forever grateful for your support and willingness to help me transform our little corner of the planet. Please, take your sustenance, but once

Tristan and I open the dancing, I expect to see you on the dance floor. Qandi, will you do the honors?"

"Oh, my Divinity. It is my supreme pleasure." He gave Phoenix a wink and strutted to the stage, leaving Tristan to wonder why everyone was behaving so strangely. Winks, little grins, Wiccan's disappearance.

"Excuse me. I'm sorry to interrupt your revelry, but I have an important and overdue introduction to make." Qandi stood at the microphone, waiting for the crowd to grow quiet. When he had their attention, he turned to Phoenix and nodded. "It is my esteemed pleasure to present our new mayor, his eminence Phoenix Ashe."

Phoenix strode to the stage, thanking Qandi before turning to the audience. "Thank you for your welcome. I appreciate all your enthusiasm and look forward to working together. Tonight is about celebrating, so rather than rehash this afternoon's speech, I want to say the ideas presented will be available on your holo-screens, pads and papers in the morning. I know you are all eager for the musicians to play, but before the dancing begins, I have something I'd like to add. Something personal, so I hope you might indulge me."

Phoenix grasped the podium's edge as a murmur rolled through the crowd. He wondered what they were thinking, as there had never been a mayoral reception where the mayor appeared with a femme on his arm. Nor had there been one filled with heteros, femmes, sapphics and hybrids as well as mascs. He hoped the eclecticism was not just a different but a welcome change.

"May I ask for Tristan Faire to join me?"

Tristan startled hearing his name and wondered what Phoenix had in mind. Terra nudged him to get him moving. He joined Phoenix on stage, trying to read his intentions only to hear him reciting children's nursery rhymes. He listened in on his mother's thoughts and was met with similar recitations. The same with Loren and Riley. *What is going on?* He turned to Phoenix and frowned, feeling like he'd stepped into an alternate universe. Maybe he hadn't yet awakened from the alley in Hybridia. Perhaps he was still lying there and hallucinating.

"Tristan, this afternoon I made promises to my constituents. I've vowed to do my part to end discrimination in our prefecture and with the Arch Prelate's help, we are removing all restrictions on marriage. Henceforth, all couples of legal majority can marry without regard to singularity, duality or genetics."

"That's a good thing. Isn't it?" Tristan whispered, confused over the need for him to join Phoenix on stage.

"Yes, love. That is a *very* good thing. There is something else though."

"What's that?"

"I would like for us—you and me—femme and masc—to be the first to wed under the new laws, if you're agreeable."

"Okay…wait…what? Did you ask me to *marry* you?"

Phoenix grinned, and Tristan wondered about the expression on his own face. Was it as stupefied as he felt? Had he correctly understood Phoenix?

"What do you say? Will you become my spouse? I swear to love you until the Divinity calls for me. I promise to be faithful to you in body and mind and to never doubt you again. May I become your husband?"

"Are you certain, Phoenix Ashe?"

"My love, I was sure the first time we transcended. I was just too stubborn and slow to admit it." Tristan stared in wonder at the strong, assured masc with the deepest, darkest eyes he'd known. Around his neck, Phoenix wore the same pendant he'd worn in the display parade. It was Tristan's color, the aqua that matched his eyes, sat luminous in the hollow of his lover's throat. The longer Tristan watched Phoenix, the darker the masc's skin became. There was no doubt of his attraction for Tristan, but was it sufficient to base a marriage? Was love enough? Tristan hesitated to answer, distracted by a persistent buzzing in his ears. He realized it was a voice. An unfamiliar articulation.

"Tristan Faire Ashe. You believe I do not bless this union? You are my chosen. Phoenix is my chosen. Your doubts are unwarranted, you have but to trust your faith in me and you will be rewarded."

"Tristan?" Phoenix placed a hand on his shoulder, and he read the doubt in his mind over the wisdom of proposing marriage to him in such a public venue. He'd never thought Phoenix might *want* to marry him. Phoenix's hand trembled on his arm as his awaited his response.

"Tristan Faire, get your head out of your nether regions and give Phoenix an answer before he passes out!" Terra's psychic shout startled Tristan from his stuporous thoughts.

He took in Phoenix's sudden pallor and the quiver of his hand squeezing his own arm. "Yes, of course I will marry you. I love you, Phoenix Ashe."

The anxious crowd let out a collective breath. Terra Gaia's joyful squeals carried across the ballroom as Wiccan Tall picked her up and swung her in circles. Loren and Riley wiped tears from their eyes. Qandi

Kane jumped on the opportunity to plant kisses on the newly engaged couple.

When he released them, Phoenix took Tristan in his arms and captured his mouth in a searing kiss.

"You scared me. I was certain you planned on refusing me."

"For a fleeting moment I thought about it, but then the Divinity spoke to me."

"She did?"

"She said we were chosen and to have faith in her and she will reward us."

"She's never wrong. Don't be afraid to follow her advice."

"And she called me Tristan Faire Ashe."

"Hmm. I love how that sounds."

In a far corner, Arch Prelate Thom Didymas watched the couple kissing on the dais surrounded by family, friends and the Divinity's children. A small smile tilted his lips at the secret he harbored.

"Well, Thom, it's a good thing—a very good thing—no one knows you're an accomplished telepath," he said, chuckling to himself before turning away to return to his rectory.

"Yes, it is my son. Your Divinity works in mysterious ways."

"That you do, Exulted One. That you do."

Want to see more from this author? Here's a taster for you to enjoy!

Beyond Heartache: Heartache and Hope
C.L. Etta

Excerpt

The restlessness grows within me, even as we sit here wrapped in each other's arms. Almost a man, I can see that my feelings for him have evolved. How can I make him recognize and accept the change? Once, I was happy to be the boy-next-door who was included in his family of two—a mother and son who loved and nurtured me as if I were the 'little brother'. Yet, although his mother will always be my Mama D, I am no longer content to be called *hermanito*, his 'little brother'. Call me *querido*, or call me your boyfriend. In turn, I will call you mine.

"Raphael?" I break the silence using his given name, rather than Raffle, the nickname I gave him when I was only eleven. Now I choose to abandon the name of our childhood and speak to him as a man, because I am a man desiring love's first taste from the banquet I hold in my embrace.

"Yes, Kevin." The languid purr of his voice sweeps through me, setting my libido on fire.

"Will you kiss me?"

"Not tonight, *herm* —"

I stop him with a touch of my fingers to his lips. *Hermanito.* Once, the word soothed me like balm applied to a burn. Now it does nothing but provoke me. His arms encircling me, keeping me safe, are not the arms of a big brother but rather the embrace of a cherished lover. As if reading my mind, he kisses my fingers and removes them from his lips. "Not tonight, Kevin. Let's sit here quietly and appreciate one another. It is enough for now."

It isn't enough—I long for more than this make-believe relationship we have created. Yes, I say 'we' because I have been a willing participant through my acquiescence. I was fearful that if I were to push for more than this enforced celibacy, he would once again ask me to leave, and this time it would destroy me. So we go on, with each night blending into the next. Even as my body burns for more, he is content with the status quo. The more content he is, the more discontented I become.

Gone is the innocent child whose happiness was defined by Raphael's contentment. Sometimes I long for those carefree days when he led without regard for what I wanted and I followed, satisfied to be in his shadow. If he was happy, I was happy. My life was centered on that mantra, which defined us. What happened to that boy? When did he change into this mass of unfulfilled wanting? There is a quiet anger kindling in my soul, its destructive tendrils seeking the impetus to burst into flame. But for tonight the fire is banked, albeit smoldering within the fragile walls of my heart.

* * * *

Several nights later, the night before my high school graduation, there's a sharp rapping on our door just as we finish cleaning the kitchen. I answer the -insistent knocking to find myself face to face with the Prince of Darkness who once dared to call himself my father. Struck dumb by his appearance on our doorstep, I stare in disbelief at Jasper Monroe, memories of his savage beating assailing me, trapping me in a dark replay of the horrific nightmare that has haunted my dreams for months…

Shouts of "Filthy fucking faggot," relentless pounding fists, and boots kicking me as I lie curled into a defenseless ball in the dark. This is a nightmare – no, this is my reality. Why? My mind screams as the never-ending beating goes on and on. Each savage blow pummels my flesh, rending me apart until there is nothing left but pain – white, blinding pain everywhere. There is only Shadow, growling outside, to hear my ear-shattering screams as each blow is underscored with words of hate…derision…revulsion.

Mercifully, the pounding stops. I hear my assailant breathing hard. He is winded, unable to continue the vicious blows. Pain meets sorrow as the truth is unveiled to me in the greatest of betrayals. My dad, it's my dad who has beaten me with such savage malice – the kind of malice I didn't know a father could have for a son – the kind of malice that destroys all trust, all love, all hope. Heartbroken, I close my eyes against the malevolence directed at me.

Shadow's menacing growl from behind me, as he is poised to attack, snaps me back to the present. Now I stand in front of the open door, my feet glued to the floor and my hand frozen to the doorknob. The glue and ice are all that keeps my quaking body from folding into itself and collapsing to the floor in terror.

"Hello, Kevin. Can I come in?"

It's such a simple request. I long to say, *No, you can't come in, you poor excuse for a father and even poorer excuse for a human being.* Anger's tendrils wrap their way around my heart, squeezing until I silently scream. *You were supposed to love me unconditionally. You can't come here and act as if nothing happened. You can't come here and shatter the fragile peace I have found. You can't come here to my home, my sanctuary.*

Instead, I say nothing as I reluctantly step back and open the door. *Noooeeeeo.* The door's squeaking hinge sounds like a grim warning. I hesitate, wondering if I shouldn't just slam the door closed, rather than subject myself to the heartache of whatever Jasper wants.

Hope is a funny thing. It's a candle that can be thoughtlessly extinguished as it had been on the night my dad beat me. Even so, a remnant is always there, lingering in the background, an ember-glowing wick, waiting to ignite. My candle of hope burned for a parent who would love me, his only child, with acceptance in his heart. It was extinguished when he beat me the night he discovered me dressed in my beloved drag.

With the tendrils of my smoldering anger and the tiny ember of hope growing within me, both battling for dominance in my heart, I study my dad as I struggle to determine if he is friend or foe. I hear the echoes of the hate-filled derision he'd spewed while continuing to kick me as I lie helpless on the floor — *"Filthy fucking faggot."* I'm about to slam the door in his face when Jasper puts his hands up to stop me.

The sight of his hand gives way to memories of our first Thanksgiving spent with Raffle and his mama. I can see my smaller hand clasped in Dad's as we'd prayed for God's blessings, and I recall the warm feelings his simple touch had evoked. With my mind still trying to reconcile his gentle touch with his vicious fists, I move out of the way and let Jasper into the kitchen where Raffle is waiting. I know Raffle will protect me from whatever Jasper wants.

"Jasper, what are you doing here?" Raffle asks with surprise written on his face as he gauges my reaction.

"I need to talk to you, son. To you and to Kevin."

I snort at his calling Raffle 'son'. He hasn't called *me* 'son' since I came to live with him. What's it been, six or seven years now? I have been 'boy', or 'Kevin', but never 'son'. The candle of hope begins to flicker as the flames of rage grow. Dispassionately, I observe as Jasper removes and carefully unfolds a paper from his pocket, setting it before him like a presidential cue card. Holding my breath, I listen as he talks. His ominous words unknowingly open the metaphorical door, allowing me to leave the confines of the closet where Raffle has kept me ever since I revealed to him that I'm gay.

Soon, I promise myself. *Soon I will go.*

Sign up for our newsletter and find out about all our romance book releases, eBook sales and promotions, sneak peeks and FREE romance books!

About the Author

With a shriek heard from sea to shining sea when her first book, Heartache and Hope, was accepted for publication, C. L. began her journey into the world of storytelling. Having raised a husband and three children, C. L. spends her free time reading and enjoying her life. After acquiring a wealth of experience in consumer and mortgage finance, software support, and nursing, C. L. is ready to nurture her creative muse.

A self-described romance novel junky who considers tequila a food group, C. L. began hearing voices and was alarmed until she realized there was a cast of characters banging around in her head, demanding their stories be told. Not wanting to let them down, she keeps her laptop nearby and her thesaurus handy.

C.L. Etta loves to hear from readers. You can find her contact information, website details and author profile page at https://www.pride-publishing.com